THE ALDEN COLLECTION

Isabella Macdonald Alden

The King's Daughter

CREATION HOUSE

LAKE MARY, FLORIDA

Creation House
Strang Communications Company
600 Rinehart Road
Lake Mary, FL 32746
(407) 333-0600

Unless otherwise noted, all Scripture quotations are from the King James Version of the Bible.

CONTENTS

ABOUT THE AUTHOR

sabella Macdonald Alden, under the pen name "Pansy," exerted a great influence upon the American people of her day through her writings. The effect of that influence was "right feeling, right thinking and right living" by the thousands of families who read her books.

Mrs. Alden coauthored some books with her sister, Marcia Macdonald Livingston. Perhaps their best collaboration was *By Way of the Wilderness*, a romance novel which influenced the later writings of her niece, Grace Livingston Hill, best-selling author of inspirational romances. "Auntie Belle" was Grace's ideal, and she and her sister Marcia served as examples to Grace of what a woman could be before God, her family and her community.

Mrs. Alden also helped her niece get started in her career. A few months before Grace's twelfth birthday in 1877, she had been listening to Grace tell a story about two warmhearted children. As she listened she typed out the story and later had it bound and printed by her own publisher into a little hardback book with woodcut illustrations. She surprised her niece with the gift on her birthday. That was Grace's first book.

Born November 3, 1841, in Rochester, New York, Isabella Macdonald was the fifth daughter and the sixth child in a family of seven children.

Her father, Isaac Macdonald, was educated, able to provide a comfortable life-style for his family and deeply interested in everything religious.

Her mother, Myra Spafford Macdonald, was the daughter of Horatio Gates Spafford (1778-1832). Spafford was well-known locally in his day for his *Gazetteer of the State of New York* (1813-1824) and textbooks on geography. But Belle's grandfather is best-known today for the hymn "It Is Well With My Soul," which he penned after his four daughters were tragically lost at sea and only his wife survived.

Belle's character flourished in an atmosphere filled with religious thought and feeling. Every experience held religious significance for her, and almost all of her actions were motivated by an evangelistic desire.

Belle and her sister Marcia were nicknamed by their father "the two queens of bedtime tales" because of the stories they told. It was probably from many of these stories that Belle gathered ideas for her books. From her father she also received the name "Pansy," when she was a very little child.

To protect her from the "foreign element" in the

crowded public schools of the mill town in which the family lived, Belle's father home-schooled her on a regular daily basis. Her guide and friend, he encouraged her to keep a journal when she was young and to develop a natural affection for writing. Under his direction she acquired the ease and aptness of expression for which her writings became known. When Belle was only ten, her composition "Our Old Clock," inspired by an accident to the old family clock, was published in the village weekly, launching her literary career.

Ten years later in 1866, while studying at the Oneida Seminary in New York, Belle wrote her first novel, *Helen Lester*, in competition for a prize. She won fifty dollars for submitting the manuscript that best explained the plan of salvation so clearly that very young readers could easily follow its teachings if they desired to and so pleasantly that they would be drawn into the Christian fold.

She completed her education at the Seneca Collegiate Institute in Ovid, New York, and the Young Ladies' Institute at Auburn.

While Belle was a student at Oneida, she was courted by Gustavus Rossenberg Alden, a young student at Auburn Theological Seminary. Ross and Belle fell in love and were married May 30, 1866, in Gloversville, New York. Her sister Marcia's husband, Charles Livingston, performed the ceremony in the Macdonald home.

Ross, a lineal descendant of John Alden, one of the first settlers in America, was ordained as a minister and served as a pastor in churches in New York, Indiana, Ohio, Pennsylvania, Florida and Washington, D.C. The Aldens moved from place to place perhaps in part to provide Belle with personal contacts and local color for her books.

Throughout her career Belle took an active interest in all forms of religious endeavors, but her greatest contributions came in her writings.

Following her success with her prize-winning first novel *Helen Lester*, Belle kept up a steady pace with her literary work. At one time her books sold 100,000 copies annually with translations in Swedish, French, Japanese, Armenian and other languages.

She usually wrote for a young audience, hoping to make religion appealing to youth and following the Golden Rule a joy. The themes of the books focused on the value of church attendance; the dangers lurking in popular forms of recreation; the duty of total abstinence from alcohol; the need for self-sacrifice; and, in general, the requisites, tests and rewards of being a Christian.

Reading was more strictly supervised for young people in that day than it was later, and Sunday schools provided many families with most of their reading material; thus, Belle's fiction received wide circulation because of its wholesome content.

Furthermore, readers liked her books. Her gift for telling stories and her cleverness in dreaming up situations, plus just a little romance, held the interest of both young and old. Belle portrayed characters and events that anyone might encounter in a small American town during the last quarter of the nineteenth century. One writer was reported to have said in 1932 that "whoever on his ancestral book shelves can discover a stray copy of one of the Pansy books will know more, on reading it, of culture in the American eighties than can otherwise be described." She was also known for developing characters who possessed an unwavering commitment to follow the Master.

Belle believed wholeheartedly in the Sunday school movement and put that belief into action. She edited a primary quarterly and wrote primary Sunday school lessons for twenty years.

From 1874 to 1896 she edited the *Pansy*, a Sunday magazine for children, which included contributions from family members and others. An outgrowth of the magazine was the Pansy societies for self-improvement, made up of young subscribers and aimed at rooting out "besetting sins" and teaching "right conduct."

For many years she taught in the Chautauqua assemblies and, with her husband, was a graduate of what was called the "Pansy Class," the 1887 Class of the Chautauqua Literary and Scientific Circle — the first book club in America. The Chautauqua assemblies were an institution that flourished in the late nineteenth and early twentieth centuries; they combined popular education with entertainment in the form of lectures, concerts and plays and were often presented outside or in a tent.

Belle's final years were marked by trials and suffering. In 1924 the Aldens' only son, Raymond, died. Amidst her responsibilities as a minister's wife, a mother and a prolific author, she had found time to play a significant role in her son's career.

That same year, after fifty-seven years of marriage, Ross Alden died. Two years later Belle was injured in an automobile accident; not long after that she fell and broke a hip. She continued writing until the end. *Memories of Yesterday*, her last work, was edited and published in 1931 by Grace Livingston Hill.

Isabella Macdonald Alden died August 5, 1930, at the age of eighty-nine in Palo Alto, California, where she and her husband had moved in 1901.

A week later Grace Livingston Hill wrote the following letter to a sympathetic acquaintance:

"Thank you for your kind sympathy in the loss of my dear aunt, Mrs. Alden. It is of course very hard to feel that she is not any longer where I may get her beautiful letters and have constant correspondence with her, for she is the last member of my childhood family to go; and it makes the world seem a lonely place and brings a great longing for the day when we shall all be together again and with the Lord Jesus Christ.

"But the sadness in my aunt's going is far outbalanced by the gladness and exultation we feel for her in being released from her pain and suffering.... She longed so to go and was such a terrible sufferer these last few years, and so brave and sweet and ready to go, that we could only be joyous even through our tears. She was very wonderful."

A sentiment echoed by the many readers who have enjoyed Isabella Macdonald Alden's books through the years.

Deborah D. Cole

CHAPTER I

DELL'S
RETURN HOME

*"What I do thou knowest not now;
but thou shalt know hereafter."*

he was dressed in a plain, neat, buff linen traveling suit and looked fresh and comfortable, despite the heat and dust of the August day. She stood in the doorway of a village railway depot, tapping the toe of one neatly booted foot on the sill of the door in a manner that might have betokened impatience or restlessness. Turning occasionally, she let her bright eyes rove over the ill-built, ill-kept, never cleaned room, where hapless travelers were doomed to pass their waiting time. She shuddered in disgust.

Up the long, dusty hill leading to the depot buildings straggled a middle-aged man, his hands in his pockets and his straw hat on the back of his head. He quickened his pace a very little when he saw the fair picture framed in the doorway and mounted the steps and stood before her. "Well, and so you are really here!"

The young lady so addressed jumped down from the doorstep. Standing beside the man, she reached up and touched her lips to his hard, brown cheek.

"Didn't you expect me, Father?"

And now it is your turn to be surprised; you would never have guessed the relationship: this little lady was so dainty and neat and graceful, and the man so rough and coarse and ungainly. He answered his daughter's question with a half laugh, half grumble: "Oh, kind of, and kind of not. Your fine folks out there have so bamboozled you up that I wasn't sure you — any of you — would remember that you had a father. Well, where's your luggage?"

"Here are my baggage checks. There are two trunks, and there's a little box besides — that's for you. Uncle Edward sent you some of Grandma's choice books."

"Thank you for nothing," the man said gruffly. "We need a thousand things more than we do books. Old rubbish, not worth paying to have 'em carried home. I've a good mind to leave 'em here to be used for firewood."

The girl's bright eyes flashed, but she spoke in a cool, quiet tone. "If you can't afford to have them carried down, Father, get a rope for me and bore a hole in the box, and I'll drag them home; I can as well as not."

Her father gave her a curious, puzzled look but seemed to make nothing of her grave face.

"Oh, I'll have 'em taken down," he said at last. "But I don't set any great store by 'em myself. Your Uncle Edward heired all the reading taste there ever was in our family. Here, you, Bill Grimes," he added, raising his voice and beckoning to a man in the distance with a cart. "Just give me a lift here, won't you? My team is away today."

The man drove around to the depot steps, where the two were busy about trunks and bundles. Whenever chance favored him, the young man gave the dainty maiden sly glances until she turned toward him and said, with frank kindness, "How do you do, Mr. Grimes? You remember me, don't you?"

He doffed his cap, awkwardly enough, while the blood mounted to his very hair and could go no further. The elder man put his hands on his fat sides and shook with laughter.

"Mr. Grimes!" he exclaimed, when he could speak. "Now if that ain't the richest note!" and he went off into another laugh. "I reckon you ain't heard that name since the old man died. Have you, Bill? Come, come, Dell, you mustn't go to puttin' on airs here. You ain't down in Boston now, you must remember."

The imperturbable calm of the young girl's face and the composure of her voice seemed to awe her father into puzzled silence. "I shall certainly try to call people by their right names, Father, here in Lewiston, just as I would anywhere else."

Her father didn't speak again until the last trunk was strapped securely to the cart. "Now we're ready. I guess you and I will jog on ahead, Dell." And they started to walk through the long, dusty, sleepy village streets.

The houses straggled at irregular and uncertain intervals, on either side of the street, and every single one of them looked as though the paint had been worn off some three generations back. There were blinds hanging by one hinge, suggestive of many a delicious creak and groan once the November wind had fair play among them. In the center of the old town stood a great weather-worn, sorrowful-looking wooden barn, by courtesy named a church. To Dell Bronson's Boston-accustomed eyes, this seemed to be the climax of the forlorn picture.

Her father glanced furtively at the still creature beside him. "How does it all look? Natural like?"

"It looks," said Dell, speaking slowly and with great gravity, "as though all the people had gone away two hundred years ago and never come back — and must have been glad of it ever since."

"Ha, ha, ho, ho!" chuckled the father. "You're a cute one, I guess. That's pretty good." And then they had reached their home.

Home! No, the wooden church had not been the climax after all. It was here in this long, low, once yellow-painted, now dirt-begrimed village tavern with wooden shutters and broken windows, a dirty piazza running the length of the building. On five wooden chairs lounged five of the most disgusting creatures that ever tilted back on the piazza of a third-rate hotel, smoking and chewing, spitting and staring.

"Well, here you are, home at last," the father said as he pushed open the great yellow door.

Home. Was it actually her home? She shivered a little, not outwardly, and sped up the uncarpeted stairs without letting herself glance at any of the objects inside that door.

The room into which she ushered herself was long and narrow. In one corner stood a single bedstead on which was mounted a feather bed with a blue and green patchwork quilt crookedly draped over it. It was an indication of Dell's character that before she removed her hat and purse, or even her gloves, she walked over to the bed and straightened the quilt, tucking it in neatly at the sides. But then she drew it out again, because on the whole the bed looked less forlorn with the quilt drooping over the sides than with it hidden away, revealing the long, narrow, ungainly rails. She fluffed up the pillows and turned down the sheets in a dainty way. She did all this before she took in the rest of the room.

There was little enough to see: a queer, old-fashioned table; a square wooden washstand with the paint worn off and one leg shorter than the others so that it tottered whenever it was touched, making a racket with the nicked washbowl and dingy pitcher; and three chairs, one a dingy rocker with a pitiful green and purple cushion on the seat. These completed the furnishing of the room, except for a faded red, green and yellow carpet, which in its best and brightest days could not have been pretty.

Dell untied the white cord that fastened the blue paper window curtain almost to the ceiling. She let the curtain fall gently, shutting out the glaring sun. Then she stepped in front of the looking glass and untied her hat, taking an earnest look at her round young face with its rosy cheeks and great bright eyes. Not so bright but that one could detect a touch of sadness in their brown depths.

She sighed again, then quickly suppressed it, thinking of a little white and green room in which she had stood only yesterday at this time. Such a gem of a room — just those two colors, from the mossy carpet that pressed her feet, to the tiny sea-green bedstead in its dress of perfect white. It had been her own room for several years. Uncle Edward and Aunt

Laura's home, but nonetheless it had seemed hers. As she brushed her hair she thought about it all.

Years and years ago — it felt like a lifetime — Uncle Edward had come and carried her away from this very room to her own green and white one in Boston. Seven years ago. Why, was it only seven? Yes, for she had been almost eleven years old, and now she was eighteen. She remembered the morning very well, and the weeks before that morning, and especially that one day on which her mother died — the pale, tired mother whose face wore only a sad, patient, gentle expression in the midst of all her discouraging surroundings. And how discouraging they were!

One day, unexpectedly, after lying for some weary weeks on a high bed in a dreary room, having very little company in her loneliness — and Dell suspected now anything but proper care — her mother died. For the first time in many years the tired woman rested, body and heart and brain.

Dell remembered it all, especially the solemn funeral, how frightened and dreary her father looked and how her tall, pale-faced Uncle Edward seemed to belong to another race of human beings. After the funeral Aunt Nancy, her father's sister, came to live with him to assume the endless cares of the dead woman, and Uncle Edward went back to his city home, taking Dell with him. Dell was his only sister's only child and had been to him in all respects as his own, though never really given up to him by her father.

Yet the years had slipped by. Once when she was nearly fourteen she came to stay a week with her father; in three days she had quarreled with Aunt

Nancy and was sent back to Boston. Otherwise she had never left the beautiful home of her adoption, where she was the carefully nurtured and much petted darling. By degrees she had nearly forgotten, until one day a letter came from her father — an unusual thing, for he was not given to letter writing. This one was brief but startling.

Dear Dell:

This is to tell you that your Aunt Nancy is dead. She died three months ago, very sudden. Since which I have rubbed along alone, and it has been pretty rubbing work. What with the sass of the girls and breaking things, I'm about sick of it. If it so be that you are of a mind to come home and do your duty by your father, why, I'll be glad to see you and will do my duty by you. But I shan't lay no demands on you. Them that has you, and has done for you, maybe thinks they has the best right to you, and if so be that you think so too, why, so be it. If you decide to come, write and let me know, and I'll come to the cars and get you.

Your obedient servant,
JONAS P. BRONSON

He closed with this signature not for any intended sarcasm, but from a vague memory that the few letters he had been called upon to write closed in that manner.

Dell read this letter standing beside her piano in

the little summer parlor in Boston, her white dress floating around her. She read at first to herself, but the shocked look on her face settled into one of such hurt that the fair-faced woman sitting in the low rocker by the window asked, "What is it, my darling?"

Dell passed the letter to her without a word.

Now the next few sentences will tell you how this young girl had been nurtured, and upon what principles her actions were founded.

The lady read the letter and then said, in quick, pained tones, "Oh, my darling child."

And Dell, still resting her hand on her beloved piano, spoke in a firm, clear voice, "Aunt Laura, when do you think I ought to go?"

A few minutes later, when Uncle Edward had joined them, he said inquiringly, "There is no question as to your duty in this matter, Dell?"

And she, raising her brown eyes to his face, answered, "Is there any room for doubt, Uncle Edward?"

"Will you tell me, my dear child, what thought you have in your heart that decides the matter for you so promptly?"

The young girl, with eyes drooping and fast filling with great tears, answered, "Honor thy father and thy mother."

So now here she was in that long, narrow room, brushing her hair before the ten-inch glass. Is it a wonder she sighed a little over the contrast? But Dell Bronson was not a girl much given to sighing. Twisting her wavy hair energetically, she addressed herself aloud, which she was rather in the habit of doing: "It isn't a palace by any means, but then it is my father's house, and I shall live in it and be happy besides, if there is any such thing."

With the expression "my father's house," a smile broke over her face, and she repeated, aloud and slowly, " 'In my Father's house are many mansions...I go to prepare a place for you.' Dell Bronson, you must not forget that your Father's house is a palace, and that you are a King's daughter. Never mind the place in which you may have to stay for a little while, just to make your preparations, you know. There are a great many things to do."

In the meantime Bill Grimes had appeared with her trunks, and they had been brought up to her room. Diving into the depths of one of them, she produced a white ruffled apron. Tying it on, she ran downstairs — more gaily than she felt, to conceal an aching desire for a loving greeting from somebody. Oh, for a mother to clasp tender arms about her!

She felt too young to begin life alone. Yet at that moment there came a bright memory to her heart of One who loved her dearly. She remembered His eternal promise, "As one whom His mother comforteth, so will I comfort you." And the forced gaiety had toned down into a true, steady brightness by the time she opened the dining-room door.

CHAPTER II

THE YOUNG MISTRESS

"Whatsoever thy hand findeth to do."

er eyes rested upon anything but an inviting picture: that long, dreary dining room with the sun pouring in blindingly through cobwebby windows, slanting its beams toward the table, which was spread for supper. Dell stepped resolutely toward that table and forced her eyes to take in all the details.

The cloth was stained with coffee and tea and daubed with egg, molasses and gravy. The sun had accomplished a melting process with the butter, and five or six flies had found oily graves. The bread, evidently cut at noon and left over, being unable to melt, had dried. Flies were holding a perfect carnival over the uncovered sugar bowls, apparently never missing those sailing around in the milk pitchers.

In a certain house in Boston there was one of the daintiest of dining rooms, with a bay window aglow with geraniums and tea roses and one great white lily. It was next to impossible that Dell should not think of that dining room and of the now vacant side where she had sat only last evening. She thought of it, but the thought did not appear in her words.

She gathered up her skirt, looked at the floor and exclaimed, "Oh, patience! I wonder if I have enough for this! It is too late to mop, but there are several other things to be done. First, though, where is Father?"

Nobody was in the dining room, and after hesitating a moment she stepped across the hall to the barroom. Five or six loungers looked at her as if she were an apparition. Confused by her unusual position, it was some minutes before she could single out her father from the group, whose feet were disposed around the room on the backs of chairs and settees. When she did, she promptly summoned him to a conference in the hall.

"Father," she said, closing the door on the staring men with disgust, "am I the housekeeper?"

Her father stared and then chuckled. "I dunno about that," he said at last. "I shouldn't wonder if Sally thinks she is."

"Who is Sally?"

"She's the cook, and you'll have to do about right if you don't want to get turned out, and like enough you'll get turned out anyhow, if her back happens to get up about anything. I've been expecting her to go, off and on, these three months."

"But, Father, I want to be housekeeper myself. I can't do anything for your comfort unless I am mistress, and I want to have things different. It isn't comfortable in there!" This she said, inclining her head toward the dining room.

Her father shrugged his shoulders expressively. "No more it ain't," he said. "I've 'most forgot the meaning of the word. Why, Dell, I ain't had no comfort since your mother died."

There was a plaintive sound to his voice that brought tears to Dell's eyes.

She placed a gentle, caressing touch on his coat sleeve. "Well, we'll have things different after a while. Then I am to be mistress, am I?"

Her father shook his head again. "I dunno about that. You must keep on the right side of Sally. And Kate — she ain't far behind, though I do think she ain't quite so boisterous like."

"Who is Kate?"

"Well, she's the chambermaid and dining-room girl and maid-of-all-work — a pretty decent kind of a girl when she ain't mad, which she is mostly."

"But, Father, I want it the other way. I want them to be trying to keep on the right side of me!"

Mr. Bronson gazed thoughtfully at the young creature before him and then laughed. "What would you do if they should both flare up and leave?" he asked, with the air of one who had presented a formidable trouble.

But her answer was prompt: "Get others in their place, of course."

"And s'pose they sass you and don't pay no attention to your notions?"

"Then I should dismiss them."

There seemed to be something refreshing to the father in his daughter's brisk, bright words and ways. He looked down at her with admiration and chuckled his answer: "You're pretty cute, I guess.

Well, fight it out with Sally and Kate, if you can. I'll back you. But you'll get sick of it and dodge and leave things go to everlasting smash, as I have." But even as he said this, he had a dim notion that this daughter of his was different from him and would be very likely to accomplish what she undertook. As he went back to that horrid barroom, he winked confidently to old Joe Simmons and said, "She's a brick, I tell you."

As for Dell, she went directly to the kitchen. Oh, the kitchen! Adjectives would fail in their attempt to describe it. Dell, on the threshold, paused and said, in an undertone of dismay, "Shall I ever be able to eat any more dinners as long as I live?" Then seeing that the two slatternly beings who occupied the space between the stove and the sink had each two sharp eyes, she stepped forward and spoke pleasantly. "How do you do? I know your names, but I don't know just which of you owns each name. Which is Sally and which is Kate, please?"

The red-haired creature answered, her arms pressed against her plump sides: "I'm Sally, and her's Kate. Do you want anything out here?"

"Several things" was Dell's prompt answer. "In the first place, Sally, I want to know if you have any clean tablecloths."

"Perhaps I has, and perhaps I hasn't. What of it?"

"Only that Kate and I want a clean one right away. We're going to set the table over again, and that cloth in there is all ready for your washtub."

Kate giggled, and Sally frowned.

"The table is set for supper," she said wrathfully. "And it is about time to have it, and it's going to be had too, and folks as doesn't belong to the kitchen had better keep out — and not spoil their fine clothes."

Dell's voice was clear and firm, yet gentle. "Then we'll delay supper for half an hour and get the table into proper order. And, Sally, I may as well explain to you now that I am Mr. Bronson's daughter, and I have come here to take charge of his house. I am very much obliged to you for doing it all the while. It must have been hard for you to have had so much care, and a great deal of work besides; but now I have come home to share the work, and I hope it will not be very hard for either of us."

Sally's face had grown ominously dark during this little speech, gracefully worded and gently spoken though it was, and at its close she burst forth: "Indeed, and I think it won't be hard for me any longer. I'll not do another stroke of work in this house. I'll not be bossed about by any red-cheeked chit like you. I'll tell you that."

Ere Sally had finished speaking, Dell's hand was in her pocket. She drew forth her purse and spoke in a calm, dignified tone: "Very well. How much do I owe you?"

Poor, cross Sally! Her favorite weapon, which she had held over the heads of so many helpless mistresses, with which she had endless times driven poor Mr. Bronson back to the barroom in despair, had never before met with such a response. She stood silent and dismayed, whereas Kate could not but start giggling again.

Dell saw her advantage and with rare diplomacy followed it up. With quiet dignity she returned her purse to her pocket and spoke gently and pleasantly: "I will overlook your improper language to me, Sally, because I see you have allowed yourself to become angry. I will even give you time to change your mind. If, after thinking the matter over, you decide you want to try to find out if we cannot get along comfortably together and be helps to each other, we will say no more about this. But if you still want to go, you may come to me tomorrow morning for your wages."

She turned to Kate with a bright smile. "Now, Kate, if you will get that tablecloth, you and I will set to work and see how soon we can get supper ready."

Dell left the kitchen in some doubt as to whether she would see either Kate or the tablecloth. But she set to work clearing the dishes to a side table, and presently Kate appeared with a beautifully clean tablecloth hanging over her arm. Dell's eyes fastened upon it in genuine pleasure. It was possible then to have something clean.

"Who does the ironing?" she asked as they spread out the cloth with its crisp, fresh folds.

"I does, mostly," Kate answered. "I irons the tablecloths."

"It is beautifully done," the young mistress said. "I never saw one look nicer than this."

Kate's face broke into a broad, pleased smile. It was new to her to hear words of commendation. She tramped briskly about, doing Dell's bidding with an air of satisfaction, and Dell, as she looked at her simple, round face, knew that Kate's heart was won.

They were very busy during the next half-hour. With some pleasant explanation, one improvement after another was suggested: the knives rubbed a little; a damp cloth taken to the glass sugar bowl; fresh milk pitchers brought; freshly cut cakes of butter on glittering squares of ice; freshly cut plates of bread; the goblets washed until they shone.

"It do make a difference," Kate said, and Dell

thought it did. She could hardly make it seem the same table she had surveyed half an hour before. A few more touches, and the supper was ready.

"Do you wait on the table?" Dell asked Kate, with many an inward misgiving as to the girl's slatternly appearance. Maggie, the girl who waited at Aunt Laura's table, was a picture of neatness. If Dell had but known it, Kate looked much better than usual, having smoothed her hair and put on a net in honor of the expected newcomer. Kate remembered it and, conscious of her superior appearance, answered blandly, "I does."

"Then I believe we're ready. Aren't we, Sally? I'll take in your tea cakes, Kate, while you roll down your sleeves, and — do you wear white aprons? You have one, haven't you? Suppose you run and get it then, and I'll ring the bell."

"La!" said Kate, with a touch of glumness. "Yes, I has one, but I don't wear it. They doesn't care. If I only gives them tea enough, and bread and butter, that's all they wants. They doesn't know whether my apron be white or black."

"Very likely," Dell said. "But then, you see, we care, and we want to have everything very nice tonight. Do you iron aprons as nicely as you do tablecloths? Run and get yours on, so I can see if you do." And Kate, to her own astonishment, went.

The tea bell rang, and the men lounged in from the barroom and piazza — among them two brisk young clerks who had just come, one from the post office and the other from the store. Dell, in the pantry just off the dining room, waited to watch Kate's movements and hear the comments.

The two clerks sat opposite each other. "I say, Tom," one of them exclaimed, "the millennium's come. Did you know it? Clean cloth, clean knives and no flies in the milk, as true as you're alive."

"Yes, and look at the butter, will you? 'Tisn't the millennium — it's paradise." This was his companion's response.

Dell heard their comments and smiled and sighed — smiled over their evident satisfaction and sighed to think that perhaps this was really their highest idea of that paradise which their tongue so lightly syllabled.

Presently her father came in, and Dell watched eagerly to see if he would note the changes. He took his accustomed seat, looked down the length of the table and then rose. Stepping out to the kitchen sink, he washed his hands. Then, disappearing for a moment, he returned with his hair brushed and a linen coat covering his soiled shirt sleeves. Dell clapped her hands over her mouth to stifle a little gasp of delight at this emphatic comment on the new order of things.

Alone in her room that night, she thought about this new life that had opened to her. She tried to shut out that fair, green room with its dainty belongings, the luxurious home in its elegant beauty. She tried to shut out the vivid contrast between the pale, refined face of her Uncle Edward and the uncultured, stolid face of her father. Failing in both these efforts, she turned resolutely away from them. Drawing from her pocket her tiny Bible, she read about that other home of hers, where they had no need of the sun in its glory, and about the other Father of hers, the shining of whose face was the light of heaven. She read until her own face shone with the reflection of all this unutterable grandeur, and earthly homes and friends faded and were forgotten.

CHAPTER III

THE LETTER AND
THE VISITOR

"I will guide thee with mine eye."

efore Dell had been at home two weeks, she received a letter one morning from her Uncle Edward. She rushed with it to her own room and fairly hugged it to her heart. She covered the soiled envelope and inky postage stamp with kisses before she set about devouring its contents. How delightfully familiar the smooth-flowing letters looked.

BOSTON, August 30, 18-

My dear Dell,

"Dear daughter" I had nearly written, so much does it seem to me that I am

31

writing to my own child. But even while I sighed to remember that you are not my daughter, and therefore not with us today, I rejoiced over the thought that you are a daughter of the eternal God and that your Father has you in His constant care and keeping.

Your Aunt Laura sends love and a wish for your presence because of canned fruit or fruit that is to be canned or something of that sort — not, of course, for any other reason. We attended the concert last evening without you. That part was sad; the concert was fine. Do you think much, during these concert days, of the great multitude clothed in white, with palms in hand, who sing with a loud voice and cease not day or night? I thought of it last evening. Your Aunt Laura leaned forward to me during one of the parts in which we had expected to hear your voice and said, "She will not be missing from the other concert. When the ten thousand times ten thousand sing the triumphal song, our Dell will join the chorus."

"There is more to it even than that," I answered her. "I trust voices will be added to that chorus — because of her not being with us tonight." Have you thought of it, Dell? Perhaps the Father called you to that part of His vineyard so you might induce some singers to join in the eternal song of the redeemed. Dear Dell, don't go to that heavenly home alone. I am sure people in Lewiston who have not yet thought about it will be glad to go with you when you press them to join you.

The thought brings me to the main reason for my writing this letter in some haste this morning, when I would normally be tending my account books. God has opened a wonderful door to you. Do you remember the sentence in your Father's letter, "No drunkard shall inherit the kingdom of heaven"? You have been carefully and prayerfully taught that truth; I think you feel it in all its fullness, and now the Father has called you to a place where this truth is unknown or disregarded — that you may work and pray that tempted feet will turn in to the narrow path.

I glory in your call, dear child. Be worthy of your commission. When He calls you home to give Him your statement of the work, be sure you have no undone duty pressing your conscience. I did not mean to preach a sermon, dear child. You know that is not my vocation. I only mean to give you little hints, here and there, of the peculiar trust the Lord must have in you to have given you this early in life so wide and solemn a working place — in His garden.

I think you have learned so well whose daughter you are and what the King expects of His children that it is unnecessary to remind you of the longing your heart should feel for your earthly father. Carry the longing constantly — to see him one day moving triumphantly among the heavenly chorus.

No, my dear Dell, that is bad advice. I mean, lay the great longing of your heart at the feet of your elder Brother. Ask His daily, hourly help.

I fear I can help you in this effort only through my prayers. Your father will hear no word from me, as that word affects his business. At present it seems wiser for me to cease from personal effort. When you have reached that point the King will make it known to you. Do not be afraid to enter doors that He has opened.

There is much to say and, as usual, very little time in which to say it. Is there less time in Boston than elsewhere? I wonder. Your class in Sunday school troubles me. They do not seem to respect Miss Terry. The truth is, she wears too much jewelry and makes too marked a difference between her own demeanor and that of her girls. Do you think it would do to give her a quiet little hint of the trouble? If she were only Dell Bronson now, I could say it to her in all frankness, and I think she would receive it. I do not mean Dell Bronson receiving a bit of truth from her Uncle Edward, but Dell Bronson receiving it from her superintendent or from anyone who meant it for her good.

You told me once that I thought too highly of you; don't allow me to. Dear Dell, grow far beyond my thinking or even hoping. There are glorious possibilities of grace to be attained — a possible flight

high enough for the ambition of an angel.
Advise me, please, in regard to Miss Terry.

Joe Turner still continues to pinch his
next neighbor black and blue every Sunday afternoon, so the neighbor says, and
refuses to show any indications of civiliza-
tion. Your Aunt Laura and I have taken
him for our special subject of prayer. At
home all is as usual, except the one great
void made by your absence. I meant this
letter to be brief, but it will not terminate.
There is no way but to cut it short. One
word about the main thought in it: If you
are at a loss as to how to proceed or which
way to turn, remember your Father's letter of full and explicit instructions. Go to it
and to Him for direction. Following this
rule there is no possibility of mistakes.

Good morning, dear child.

Your loving uncle

Dell folded the letter with a look of eagerness and
dismay. There was a little rush of tears to her eyes,
but she brushed them away quickly.

"What a singular letter that would be if it came
from anyone in this world but Uncle Edward!" she
said to herself. "The idea of congratulating me upon
the door opened for me!"

To her the door of temperance seemed shut and
bolted and barred. Who ever heard of the daughter
of a rumseller living in a hotel preaching temperance? Dell's cheeks glowed at the thought, and her
lips quivered, yet this was the undeniable fact, and
such was her nature that she had to face disagreeable

truths plainly and firmly in order to endure them at all.

What on earth could she do? It would do no good to beg her father to give up a money-making business. Hadn't her poor mother begged for that every day of her life? She wished her uncle had been more explicit.

She paced up and down her room now with a look of perplexed thought. The letter had aroused the one great burden always crouched at her heart. Her father was a rumseller — a respectable, licensed drunkard-maker. She, Dell Bronson, who had been brought up in her uncle's house to abhor the sight of liquor, to refuse its use in any shape or form, to work and plan and pray for its banishment from the civilized world, must every day face an army of rum-drinkers, must hear their silly jokes as she passed through the halls, must lie awake at night and listen to their drunken songs or quarrels or oaths, must pass by homes made wretched by the daily presence of the demon. As she faced these sights and sounds she must remember that her father furnished the poison at so much a glass, must watch his own face grow redder, his eyes more bleared, his steps more uncertain every day, and yet be powerless to help.

Did she remember that fearful sentence, "No drunkard shall inherit the kingdom of heaven"? Oh! Did she not? Sometimes it seemed written in letters of fire all over the walls of this licensed hotel. How much Dell hated that word *licensed* nobody knew. "No drunkard," and her father not only made drunkards, but the law pronounced it a legitimate business. How can license give a man the right to ruin just as many fellowmen as he possibly can, provided he pays for the privilege a few dollars a year?

Her heart sickened at the thought of all this and at the added anguish that her father had bought the privilege of barring his own soul out of heaven, as well as the souls of others.

"What does Uncle Edward think it possible for me to do? Why didn't he tell me? If he only realized, as I do, that I can do nothing, nothing." Then her eye fell on the closing lines in the letter: "If you are at a loss as to how to proceed, which way to turn, remember your Father's letter of full and explicit instructions. Go to it and to Him for direction. Following this rule there is no possibility of mistakes."

As she reread the words, gradually the look of pain died out from her face, and there came first a calm and then a smile. Uncle Edward was right. Her Father must have something He intended her to do, else He would not have called her to this wretched place.

She unclasped her little Bible, not with any definite end in view, for she knew she had no time just then to search for directions, but from a habit she had of picking up the book and just glancing at some earnest word or loving praise. But her whole face flushed and her eyes brightened as they caught the words: "I will instruct thee, and teach thee, in the way which thou shalt go: I will guide thee with mine eye."

The promise was not new to her. It just suddenly came home to her heart with that wondrous power that every lover of the Bible understands. Dell shut her Bible and dropped to her knees. The first sentences of her prayer were: "My Father, it is enough. I yield myself to You. Instruct and guide me as You will. Lead where You will. Your daughter is ready to follow. Ah, dear Father, perhaps I am not, I don't know, but make me willing. Make me all that You would have me be."

Five minutes later she was summoned to the tearoom to see a caller. This same tearoom deserves a word on its own account. It was an emanation of Dell's brain, not the room exactly, but its belongings and uses. It was a little square room with a side door leading into the yard. It had been bare of furniture and appropriated to no better use than to serve as a sort of general storeroom for umbrellas, overcoats, hats, rubber boots, shawls — anything that might be needed on a rainy day. Dell had seized upon it, banished the rubbish to appropriate dark closets, dragged to light enough carpeting to cover its bit of floor, hung the windows in cream color, repapered the walls, brought from the attic an old table with three legs, coaxed the hostler into adding a fourth, covered it with an old cream-colored curtain, brought from her mother's room an old worn chair, stuffed and padded its back, seat and sides and dressed it in cloth of the same creamy tint. She had filled the window seat with little pots of sweet-smelling flowers brought from her Boston home, strewn the table with inviting books and altogether converted the former storeroom into one of the sunniest and quietest of little rooms that her father at least had ever seen.

Dell, in writing to Aunt Laura about it, said: "I call it the tearoom for reasons that I will explain to you when my plans are fully developed. But, between you and me, it might be more appropriately called the trap room, and I mean it to wage war against that fearful barroom. *How* shall, with many other things, be told you hereafter."

It had cost her two days of hard labor. Her last act had been to lay the two daily papers Uncle Edward had sent her on the little cream-colored table and inform her father, when she called him to survey the room, that he would always find the latest papers on that table and the armchair vacant at any hour of the day. So when she entered the room on this particular morning and beheld her father seated cozily in the armchair and tearing the wrapper from the late paper, she flushed with pleasure and felt that her trap had commenced its work.

Her caller was a wee sprite of a child, daintily done up in a piqué dress, with blue ribbons floating at her waist and among her brown curls. Small and sweet, with a winning ladylike shyness (and her voice as clear as a flute's), she looked with truthful blue eyes into Dell's brown ones and said: "If you please, Miss Bronson, will you sign my temperance pledge?"

CHAPTER IV

THE FATHER'S DAUGHTER

"Thou art my Father, my God."

ell looked with amused eyes on the little girl and then glanced toward her father. Evidently he had heard the little lady's petition, for he shook out his paper with a disgusted air and muttered something that his daughter could not catch.

For one moment she stood irresolute. It was an odd place to come to for signers to a temperance pledge, but the innocent little morsel looking up at her did not appreciate the difficulties. Dell's mind was very promptly made up. The first thing to do had come to her, and she meant to do it.

"Certainly I will sign it," she said in a bright voice. "Why, you have several names here already. Well, I will put mine down, and then you will have seven." She moved toward the writing table.

41

Her father spoke suddenly and more sternly than he had ever spoken to her: "Dell! What tomfoolery are you about now?"

Dell waited until her rapid fingers had left the name "Dell Bronson" in unmistakably clear letters before she answered: "I'm signing a temperance pledge, Father."

"Temperance, fiddlestick!" Mr. Bronson said. Dell folded the pledge and returned it to the little maiden. "Are you going to put your name on that thing?" he asked.

"I have done so, Father."

"Well, it is a pretty business for you to be about, I should think. You ain't in Boston now, and I reckon you better remember it. If your Uncle Edward hasn't taught you anything but to go against your father in this fashion, you may as well go back to him. I won't have such doings going on here, and you may as well know it first as last!"

The little girl dressed in the cream piqué cast a frightened glance at the surly-looking man, thrust the pledge into her mite of a basket and moved briskly toward the door.

Dell bowed and saw her out, promising, in an undertone, to be present at the evening meeting if she could. She came back to her father. Mr. Bronson had taken up his paper, but he still grumbled. Waxing louder as he received no answer, at last his words became distinct again. "Do you know what you are about?"

"I'm dusting and rearranging this table. What is the matter, Father?"

"Matter! Don't you know enough to realize that these meddling fools, who are sneaking around with pledges and coaxing folks to come to their confounded meetings, are trying to ruin my business?"

"No, sir, that isn't their object. They're trying to save drunkards."

"Save fools!" he said, and Dell answered, "Yes, sir. They are undoubtedly fools, or they wouldn't need saving. But that's what we are trying to do."

"I don't choose to have a girl of mine make a fool of herself."

"No, sir, I haven't the slightest intention of doing so. I have signed the pledge, you know."

The newspaper was flung to the floor at this point, and the rough father said: "You talk like a fool! You had no business to put your name to that paper."

Dell turned from her dusting and looked with two bright, steady eyes at her father. "Why not?"

"Why not? Don't you know I get my living, and yours, by selling rum?"

Truly Dell knew that — knew it to her bitter sorrow and shame. Her cheeks flushed, but she answered, "Yes, sir."

"And you want to help break down my business, do you? Pretty way to treat the business that clothes and feeds you!"

"Father," said Dell, "do you want me to sell rum?"

"No, of course not," he said testily. "Nobody asked you to sell anything. What I want is — "

But she quietly interrupted him. "Do you want me to drink it?"

And then there came to the father a sudden shiver as he fancied this bright, handsome daughter of his standing in his barroom drinking his liquor. He snarled his reply: "No, I don't."

"Very well, sir. I've simply promised not to do either. That is what I meant by signing the pledge. It is not, by any means, the first one I have signed. I am very sorry that rum-selling is your business. I would be willing to live on bread and water, and work hard for that, if you would give it up. I am not in sympathy with it in the least. I expect to do everything in my power to hinder the sale and the use of rum. I don't mean to use it in any possible form. I mean to talk against it and work against it and pray against it as long as I live."

There — the words were out. She had resolved on a very straightforward course in speaking of this subject with her father when the time came. She knew she would have to go contrary to his views in many ways — but nothing perhaps more frequently than in this matter. It surely was best to show her colors decidedly at this first opportunity and await the consequence.

Her father was much less angry than she had supposed he would be. He knew much better than she did the very low ebb at which the temperance cause stood in the village. He knew he had supporters many and strong. He did not in the least fear the influence of the temperance people. They irritated him, but he contented himself with calling them "fools" and "fanatics" and sneering at their efforts, which indeed were faint and weak enough almost to call for sneers instead of commendation, even from friends of the cause.

Dell's outburst half angered, half amused him. She looked so pretty standing there before him, and so utterly harmless, that he could certainly afford to laugh.

"Mighty becoming your hysterics are to you. I s'pose that's the reason your uncle trained you in 'em. He always had an eye for them kind of things. Well, well, you must have something to do, I s'pose, and I've no kind of objection to your amusing your-self in this fashion if you want to, so long as you don't plague me about it. An awful sight of good you'll find your talking and thinking and what not will do, and folks will call you a fool for trying to knock out your own underpinning. But that's nei-ther here nor there if you're suited." And having talked himself into comparative good humor, Mr. Bronson left the room.

Dell stood where he had left her, looking after him. She drew two or three quick breaths. This, then, was her father! It rushed upon her with new and over-whelming force, the gulf between them. There was no common ground on which they met. In not one single thing could they seem to sympathize. Oh, to be at home once more in her own beautiful room, to feel herself again the center and joy of her uncle's home, to escape from these surroundings: the great hot kitchen with its cross Irish girls, the dining room, with all the rough, ungainly set gathered there to eat and stare, that awful barroom with the smoking, spitting, drinking crew! Couldn't she go? How they missed her there in that beautiful home.

Who would miss her here? Her father would not object to her going back. Indeed she had a vague feeling that he disliked the sort of restraint he almost instinctively put upon himself in her presence. She knew that in some respects he was almost afraid of her. She knew she would only have to go to him with a determined air and announce her intention of re-turning to Boston by the afternoon train. He would stare and frown a little, then grumble, and perhaps even swear, but it would end in sending Joe to the cars with her trunks. She knew her being Uncle Edward's adopted child was too thoroughly under-

stood to have her movements absolutely forbid-
den — or even closely questioned. Should she go?
The thought, the possibility, made her heart beat
hard and fast, and for a moment it seemed to her that
she must go at once — that very hour.

But then. Ah, me! How all the difficulties and
reasons why rushed in the moment she lifted the
gate and let in that innocent-sounding "but then."
She looked around that cheery little morning room
brought to pass by her skill and determination. How
pure and sweet, in the very center of this dreary old
tavern. Must there not be something refining in the
atmosphere and surroundings of the room? This
little bit of her Boston home, set down here?
Wouldn't he feel the difference after a while? She
thought of the dining room, clean and neat, almost
bright now. What a dreadful room that first time she
looked in on it! The thought of the changes wrought
in the kitchen — of the wine she had banished from
the pudding sauces; of the brandy bottle filled for
culinary purposes, that she had deliberately
smashed. Certainly very little could be gained so
long as the hated poisons were so freely poured at
the table, but there were at least two of the men who
did not drink liquor at the table. They at least would
not have the taste for it fostered by the food they ate.
She had made numerous other changes and contem-
plated more.

And, besides all this, was he not after all her very
own father? Should she desert him? She who that
very morning prayed so earnestly to be helped and
guided? Should she really yield the struggle and run
back to rest and peace? No, she wouldn't. He was
her father, ignorant and coarse though he was. Despite the chewing, the spitting, the smoking and the

drinking, though his clothing and body were so permeated with the fumes of tobacco, though his breath was so choked with the fumes of liquor that it made her faint to go near him — still she was his only child. There was no possibility of getting away from that fact.

How lovingly she had seen some daughters lean on their fathers' arms; how reverently she had heard them pronounce the dear name! Her heart ached with the longing and the hopelessness. And then suddenly over this gloom there broke Dell's rich, sweet smile. A sudden thought had pressed home to her heart, a mingling of sweet and true and wonderful words, breaking up the sadness: "My Father, Thou art the guide of my youth."

Did an angel whisper those words in her ear? She had longed for a father to lean upon, such as she had known other girls to have. She had sighed bitterly over her low estate. She had forgotten for a moment whose child she was. The King's daughter! She must not forget that. Truly she had a Father whom not only all the earth but all heaven adored. Oh, yes! She could ask counsel of her Father. She could be guided by Him in all things. He could not be mistaken. He would never die and leave her. He would never, never take His supporting arm away from her. Surely she could smile and be glad.

"She's a sharp one," Mr. Bronson told himself as he walked toward the barroom. "Let her have her notions. Who cares? Don't hurt nobody. Won't do to treat her as if she was a baby or a common kind of a girl — for she ain't, that's so. She'll be scooting off to Boston first thing I know if I don't mind my p's and q's, and I should miss her, now that's a fact. Things ain't never gone so smooth-like in this house, not since her mother died. As for them silly notions about temperance, she can't do no harm, and she'll get over 'em. I'll be easy with her. All girls have 'em. They think it makes 'em big and independent. Besides, I don't want her to drink. It's a nasty habit for women. I never kept no womankind about me that would drink. I won't have 'em. I don't think it's decent." Mr. Bronson drew himself up virtuously and went straight to the bar and prepared himself a glass of brandy.

As for Dell, she went to the kitchen and made her father the daintiest little pudding that milk and eggs and sugar and fruit, beaten and mashed and otherwise mysteriously compounded, could produce.

CHAPTER V

THE MEETING

"Who hath despised the day of small things?"

ll the while Dell was dressing for the temperance meeting, she felt pleasure at the thought of meeting friends and co-workers. She had been used to many friends and much hearty work. She would accompany her Uncle Edward to the great hall in Boston and mingle there with a throng of eager workers. She liked the whole of it — the music, the brilliant lights, the enthusiastic people, the eloquent speakers. She had missed it all. She was glad to enter into it again with all her heart.

She thought about it as she walked briskly down the village street toward the church. Thought about it until her hand was on the doorknob and she pushed open the door. Then what a sudden coming down from the clouds it was! Instead of the great hall, brilliant with light and alive with well-dressed people amid the subdued tremble of wonderful music, there was that dingy, dusty, dismal church, smelling as if the united breaths of the worshippers of a hundred years back were entombed there. It was lighted by those sputtering, hissing, smoking kerosene lamps. The audience was composed of five boys, two of whom were playing football with their caps; a young man, who was preparing with the aid of his jackknife and a bit of chip to trim the aforesaid lamps; two girls, who whispered and giggled in one of the dark corners; and the dainty little bundle in piqué, Dell's morning acquaintance.

Now Dell knew that the village was very different in many respects from Boston. She knew it boasted of no public hall, and certainly the tumbledown old church building was far enough from deceiving her as to its condition. But then she had lived all of her grown-up life in Boston, and public meetings of any sort had to do in her mind with gas-illuminated buildings and swelling organs and throngs of people. She had considered them necessities.

She stood still by the door, trying to take in the situation. What a bewildering disappointment! Where was the meeting? Where were the people who would make it up? At last she did what Dell was very apt to do on trying occasions — she laughed, not very loud, but merrily. The ludicrousness of the whole thing and the absurdity of her own expectations had just crept over her. Her laugh ended, she cast about her as to ways and means. She brought the game of hat-ball to a sudden termination as she addressed the larger of the two boys: "Excuse me. Is your name Johnny?"

"No, ma'am," he said, wondering but respectful.

"It's Tommy, though."

"Well, Tommy Though, what do you suppose is the reason that you and I don't open some of these windows? How long do you suppose it will be before we bake, if we stay in this oven?"

"I don't know," he answered, laughing. "But my name's Tommy Truman."

"Mine is Dell Bronson, and I'm very glad to meet you. But about the windows. Aren't we equal to them? Is your name Tommy too?" This to the younger boy, who turned toward her with a jaunty but not ungraceful bow, and answered: "I'm Bob Mason, at your service, ma'am."

"Thank you. Then you want to know how you can serve me, of course. If you will go to the other side of the church and open every window, I shall consider myself delightfully served."

He started at once but suddenly turned back with a puzzled air. "How shall I keep them up? There's no fastenings or anything."

"Hmmm," Dell said, wrinkling her brow in feigned bewilderment. "I'm sure I don't know. It shall be part of your service to find out."

The boy laughed but went at once to work, and Tommy Truman was dispatched to the row of windows on the opposite side. Meantime the lamps, after infinite pains and some burning of fingers, were trimmed and sputtered less, but looked dim and threatening. The young man turned to Dell.

"Good evening. I shall have to introduce myself. My name is Homer Nelson. I'm bookkeeper at the factory. And you are Miss — ?"

"Bronson, from the hotel," Dell explained.

"I beg pardon," he said, with a little flush on his face. "You are not connected with Mr. Bronson who keeps the hotel?"

"I am his daughter," Dell answered quietly. Then, her eyes gleaming with mischief, "Where is the temperance meeting, Mr. Nelson?"

"Don't you see it?" Mr. Nelson said, indicating the five boys and three girls and answering the roguish look in her eyes with a frank laugh. "Don't you know about this enterprise, Miss Bronson?"

"Not in the least, except that a little mite of a child invited me to attend a temperance meeting tonight, and I have come to attend it."

"And you don't find it," laughed Mr. Nelson. "Well, it's in the process of manufacture. Let me tell you about it." He steered her to a seat, then sat down beside her, his face now thoughtful.

"Well, if you reside here, Miss Bronson, you know how completely this village is given over to rum. I have never seen anything like it in a place of its size. I have not been here long, but long enough to get the heartache over some of the scenes I have witnessed. I have a class in the Sunday school and some little influence over the boys who compose it. I determined to make an effort in the way of a temperance society. I drew up a pledge and got my boys to sign it, and two or three of their sisters signed. Then I prepared a pledge for each one and sent them out after recruits, telling them to invite everyone they saw to sign the pledge and attend the temperance meeting this evening. I had some hope of seeing enough present to form a society, and, while we all work for temperance, at the same time try to interest the people in a literary effort of some sort."

"And this is the result," said Dell, looking around on the eight small people waiting to see what was going to be done with them. While they waited, they whispered together and giggled every few minutes.

"This is the result," Mr. Nelson repeated with gravity, folding his arms and taking a survey of his audience and the room in general. He caught Dell's eye, and both of them laughed.

"Small potatoes and a few in a hill," quoted Mr. Nelson.

"Tall oaks from little acorns grow," she responded, ignoring the potatoes. "Mr. Nelson, where is your pastor?"

Mr. Nelson's moustache, and the lip under it, curled very slightly as he answered: "I have his sympathies. He hopes I will succeed and be able to do a good work. He is at Deacon Elliot's playing croquet with Miss Emmeline."

"Oh, he is. What is the reason of all that? I mean, why isn't he here?"

"Because, in the first place, Deacon Elliot doesn't approve of temperance societies, thinks pledges are an infringement of personal liberty, etcetera, etcetera; and Esquire Burton believes in using the good things of this life without abusing them, and one of the good things is whiskey; and Mr. Traverse is an unqualified supporter of the antitemperance cause; and these three are the prominent men of the church and the village. And, lastly, our pastor himself thinks good hard cider is an excellent thing. Have I given you reasons enough?"

"Plenty, and introduced your pastor to me too."

"I don't want to slander him," Mr. Nelson said earnestly. "He is a good man. I sincerely believe him to be one; only he thinks on this subject as too many good people do."

Dell's spirits, which had plummeted on her entrance into the dreary room, began to rise as difficulties thickened around her.

"Well," she said, looking with determined eyes into Mr. Nelson's face, "let us have a temperance society, Mr. Nelson, and succeed. Will you let me be your coadjutor?"

"I shall be most thankful for any assistance in any form. Under the present highly encouraging circumstances, what would you advise?"

"What was your idea? A literary society?"

"Something of that sort — the two combined, you know."

"Well," she said, spoken with that inimitable little dash of energy that made one hopeful of results, "let us have a literary society by all means."

"Of what?" said Mr. Nelson with a comical sigh.

"Of the material at hand, to be sure. Little Curly, come here, dear." Thus summoned, the little morsel in cream piqué came forward from her shy corner by the door, coaxed on by a bright smile and winning gesture from Dell.

"This is the little lady whose pledge I had the honor of signing this morning," she said as she stooped and placed a protecting arm around the little one.

"This is Mary Cobb, one of our faithfuls," said Mr. Nelson.

Dell smiled. "Dear Mary, don't you know a nice little verse to say to me?"

"I know 'Jesus loves me,' " the little girl said.

"The very thing! Will you say it for me?"

And the old church was very still. Neither whispering nor giggling went on while the sweet child voice repeated that gem of child poetry:

Jesus loves me, this I know,
For the Bible tells me so.

"That was very sweet," Dell said, secretly encouraged; her ear had caught that peculiar, clear, round sound that told her she had found a rare thing — one who could recite poetry well and naturally.

"It was very sweet indeed. And you said it just as I thought you would. How old are you, little one?"

"Almost seven."

"So I thought. Now will you ask Mama to let you come and see me tomorrow? Ask her to let you come at four o'clock and stay an hour. I have something very beautiful to teach you."

The child agreed to do so, and with a kiss and a smile she was dismissed. Dell turned triumphantly to Mr. Nelson.

"I have an exquisite piece of poetry to teach her, and she will recite it beautifully. I knew she would from her eyes. So much is arranged for."

"What next?" asked that gentleman in an amused tone. He seemed to have slipped into a subordinate position and left this bright young lady at the head.

"Oh, a declamation we must have next. Mr. Nelson, that lamp nearest you smokes horribly. I don't think you know quite as much about lamp-trimming as you might. Now where is our Tommy Truman? He can speak a piece for us, I think."

She turned to look for him, praised the ingenious arrangements by which he had contrived to make all the windows stay up, and by skillful questioning learned the extent of his oratorical powers. Finally she came gleefully back to Mr. Nelson to announce the whole matter successfully arranged. Meantime, his season of discouragement having passed, he entered with energy into the preparations and brought forward the giggling girls to present to Dell. They proved to be young misses of fourteen who were thoroughly imbued with the spirit of temperance and quite capable of doing something besides whispering and laughing, if only there could be found people wise enough to set them to work. The election of president, secretary and the like was by unanimous consent postponed until the next meeting, which was appointed for a week from that evening.

"But what shall we do for an audience?" Mr. Nelson asked at last in dismay. "We are all performers. Where are the listeners?"

"Oh, we'll have listeners," Dell said, with an emphasis that seemed to decide the matter. "In the first place, here are one, two, three — here are ten of us. How many will promise to bring one friend with them next Friday evening, as many more as they can, but one certainly, if it is possible?"

Up went her own hand in token of promise. Mr. Nelson promptly took the hint and raised his, and all the others followed their example.

"Then there will be twenty at least. Oh, we'll do very nicely. Ten is not such a poor audience, Mr. Nelson."

Her sparkling eyes traveled over the small group gathered there in the dingy church, and she added: "I'm not sure but this is the nicest temperance meeting I ever attended. It's the funniest, anyway. Tommy, will you be a gentleman and see me home?"

And as Mr. Nelson stood in the doorway of the old church and watched the boy walk proudly down the moonlit street with the young lady leaning on his arm, he felt he would have been perfectly willing to perform that gentlemanly deed himself.

CHAPTER VI

THE SQUALID HOME

"I know thy works, and where thou dwellest,
even where Satan's seat is:
and thou holdest fast my name...."

hey walked briskly down the street until they neared one of the tumble-down shanties, which had a way of appearing right in the midst of more pretentious buildings, looking more wildly out of place than they would have had they been somewhat isolated.

"Dear me!" said Dell. "What a house! What a place to live in! How should you like to have such a broken-windowed den as that for a home?"

"I shouldn't like it at all," Tommy said emphatically.

"Well, between you and me, I don't believe the people who live there like it either — not in the least. When you get to be a man, Tommy Truman, and have a family to take care of, if you go and live in such a way that by and by you have to move your family into such a rickety old hovel as that, why, I shall be dreadfully disappointed in you."

"I never shall, you may depend," said Tommy, bristling with determination.

"I'm glad you are so decided about it," Dell answered. "Because now you will be likely to set about keeping out of such places; set about it right away, I mean. Things don't happen all at once, you know. They begin to get ready away back, years and years before we think about them. I have a fancy that even that old house didn't come into this wretched condition all at once. Perhaps there was a time when all the lights were in the windows."

"I know there was," Tommy said. "When that old fellow moved in here there wasn't a pane of glass gone, and things looked kind of decent. I remember the night Sam smashed the first one. He jammed his fist right through it and made it bleed like sixty too."

Further explanation from Tommy was checked by sounds of banging and scuffling issuing from the said house. Finally a scream, full of mingled terror and anger, stopped their footsteps and made Dell's heartbeat quicken.

"What can be the matter?" she said anxiously, as they stopped and peered back at the house they had just passed.

"Oh, Sam is drunk, I suppose," Tommy said with contempt. "He is most every night of his life, and he tears around like a madman. He's got a little girl only six years old, and he whips her like all possessed. He'll kill her some time, folks think."

"He's whipping her now," said Dell, as the distinct sounds of blows and screams came out to them on the evening air. "Tommy, this is dreadful! Can't anything be done? Can't you and I do something?" and she turned and ran back toward the house.

"Miss Bronson," Tommy said, "we can't do anything with him. When he's drunk, he's just like a crazy man. Folks are afraid to go near him."

Nevertheless he followed her back to the door. Dell had her hand on the latch, and, by way of answering, she said, "Why, it's our Sam. I can see him through the window." She pushed open the door and entered.

"Ain't you awful afraid?" asked Tommy, quaking even to the toes of his new boots while at the same time itching for an adventure.

But Dell addressed her next remark to the man inside. "Why, Sam Miller! Now aren't you ashamed of yourself?"

The scene that met her eyes was appalling: a drunkard's squalid home, his wife cowering in a corner, alternately weeping and screaming while her husband held by the shoulder with iron grip their young child and struck blows with the round of a chair on the bare neck and arms and the yellow head of the shrieking girl. Not an unusual picture in the least, you perceive; in fact, a commonplace one. It was not new to Dell, for with her Uncle Edward she had penetrated into all sorts of fearful spots where people huddled and called themselves at home, for this wretched rum was to be found in Boston as well as in Lewiston.

But one feature of it was new to her — and quite sufficiently striking. It was the first time she had beheld such a picture having a vivid sense that her father was the artist of it. Hitherto Dell had shuddered with horror and mentally expended her burning indignation on some unknown and terrible villain who had sold the rum. But didn't she know only too well where Sam Miller procured his poison? He was a habitual hanger-on at her father's tavern, a regularly engaged help, bringing for her use innumerable pails of water and papers or anything she chose to send him for in the course of the day — and receiving his payment in rum.

Meantime Sam Miller eyed her glaringly and with dangerous menace at first. Then, as there stole over his bewildered senses a dim notion of who she was, a faint memory of the innumerable kind words and pleasant smiles she had bestowed on him during the last ten days must have crossed his brain, for the angry glare gave place to a sheepish side glance. Muttering something about the young imp needing a whipping every hour, he thrust her from him and stumbled up the rickety stairs out of sight. Then a curious scene ensued. Dell, having met with unexpected success, turned to comfort the wife, who had caught up her child the moment she was released. To her astonishment Dell encountered angry eyes and tongue.

"And what kind of manners do you call it for a fine lady to burst into a man's own house in the night, when he's correcting his girl, and ask him if he ain't ashamed of himself? It's yourself I am thinking might be ashamed, seeing you've no more manners than that."

Dell was silent with amazement. Not so with Tommy. He burst forth with fiery indignation: "Now, Mary Miller, that's the meanest thing out. You wanted little Mamie killed out and out, I s'pose? He'd have done it with a few more thumps, and you go and come down on the lady that saved her life!"

A great sob burst from the woman's throat as she

went eagerly about ministering to the suffering child. But her voice retained all its bitterness.

"I don't care," she muttered. "Them as thrives by the thing that makes a madman of him ain't the ones to ask him if he's ashamed. He ain't himself, Sam ain't. He wouldn't hurt Mamie more'n he would his own self, nor so much, if he knew what he was about. And it's her and hers that's made him what he is. I know who she is and who her father is, and I hate 'em both. I know how she gets her fine clothes and things. My Sam, and lots of others, gets them for her, and she needn't flaunt them here in my face and tell my Sam to be ashamed of himself. I won't stand it. I won't — so now." And the hard voice broke down in great, bitter tears that seemed wrung from her against her will, each with a groan.

Poor Dell! Poor sad-hearted girl — standing there in her youth and beauty, with her white robes floating snowily around her. What an aching heart they covered! She stood for a moment after the voice ceased, transfixed by the sting of the hard words, until Tommy's voice roused her.

"Come, Miss Bronson, don't stay where people don't know enough to tell a friend from an enemy."

Instead Dell went to the woman's side and spoke rapidly: "Mrs. Miller, if you put cold water on the child's head and bathe the lumps in ice-cold water, it will keep them from swelling and relieve the pain. And, Mrs. Miller, you are mistaken about me. I hate it, this awful business, this selling of poison, with such a hatred as I haven't words to express. I am fighting against it and praying against it, and I will do so as long as I live." Then she turned and left the house. They walked along the deserted street in silence until they neared the tavern.

Tommy broke the stillness. "Miss Bronson, don't feel bad about what that woman said. She was half crazy, you see, and she don't know anything, anyhow."

Dell smiled drearily and gave her attention to the three or four men who were staggering along the street, having just issued from her father's hospitable doors.

"Oh, Tommy, Tommy!" she sighed. "We need a temperance society, don't we?"

"Yes, we do," he said, when he would have liked to comfort her heart with the assurance that nothing of the kind was needed.

Dell replied with solemn eagerness: "Well, Tommy, let us have a temperance society, one that will be worth something. Let you and me work for it with all our might, in every way that we can think of. Let us talk about it wherever we go and to whomever we see. And let us pray about it a great deal. Will you do it, Tommy?"

And Tommy, standing there in the moonlight, took off his hat and answered with very grave and earnest words: "Yes, Miss Bronson, I will. Just as sure as my name is Tommy Truman, I will do everything I possibly can."

Dell let herself into the dismal house and paused with a kind of fascinated shudder at the barroom door. The loungers had dropped off into silence and drowsiness earlier than usual, and their deep-snoring breaths, mingled with the sizzling of the kerosene lamp, made the only sounds audible. Tilted back in his armchair, his feet on one of the tables, sat her father, snoring with the rest — his face more red and bloated than ever before. What light there was shone full on his thin hair, singling out from among the black locks many a white hair, telling of fast-coming age and swift decay. And he was her father — that bloated, disfigured being! She turned and ran from the dreadful sight up to her own room and turned the creaking button to fasten herself in. She struck a light and, dropping into her little sewing chair, gave herself up to something as near despair as Dell Bronson's cheery nature ever reached.

It is all true, she thought bitterly — just as that poor woman said. I am a rumseller's daughter! It must seem to lookers-on as though the very clothes she wore were bought with the price of misery, such as she had seen that night. But what could she do? Her hands were tied.

"If Uncle Edward realized how it is, he would see that I can do nothing," she said out loud. "It would be better for me to give up all public attempts, at least. What perfect mockery it must seem to people to have me mixing myself up with a temperance society! I live in a rum tavern, and my father sells the rum with his own hands. Yes, and drinks it too. Why, tonight if he were to try to walk, he would stagger along just like his patrons. Oh, Father, Father! Why must I have such a one? There are such good fathers in the world." And there Dell's words broke into sobs.

The storm of tears lasted for but a few minutes, however. After a while she began to move around the room, gathering into their places the things she had flung from her when she entered and otherwise tidying the place for the night. During the few weeks she had been at home, she had wrought many changes in the room. The blue paper curtains had given place to white muslin. The bed was spread in white, as was also the little toilet table. Many little feminine touches had softened its hard corners and given it a look of home.

Composed now — though still downcast — she took her little Bible and opened to the mark for her few verses of evening bread. She was reading in the book of Jeremiah, and yesterday's date was placed after the tenth verse of the twenty-ninth chapter, so the reading commenced:

"For I know the thoughts that I think toward you, saith the Lord, thoughts of peace, and not of evil, to give you an expected end. Then shall ye call upon me, and ye shall go and pray unto me, and I will hearken unto you."

She paused. Could her heart read more than those two verses just then? "And ye shall go and pray unto me, and I will hearken unto you." Here was the King Himself speaking to her, and such words!

Dell carried the words with her to her rest that night. And, though her heart was heavy, as she dropped into sleep she murmured a prayer that the Father might indeed give her "an expected end."

CHAPTER VII

THE CHILDREN'S
CLASS

"Enter not into the path of the wicked."

ell Bronson stood in the cupboard that served as a hall for the dismal church, pretty well squeezed up against the wall to be out of the way of the people. She fanned herself vigorously, waiting for the congregation to pass by and for what would come next. She looked remarkably pretty standing there in her Boston-made suit of white lawn, belted with blue and with a blue sash at her throat. Aunt Laura had been fastidious as to her darling's appearance, and to Dell it had almost been made to appear a Christian duty to look fresh and neat and as pretty as she conveniently could.

The young people of Lewiston seemed to think she looked very nice or very something, for they stared at her in a manner that made her cheeks burn.

Some of them said she had altogether too much style on for only a tavern keeper's daughter. In point of fact she was very simply and inexpensively dressed. There were silks rustling by her that cost almost as much per yard as her whole suit did, for there were expensive silks worn even in Lewiston by people who every Sabbath seated themselves in some forlorn old pew of the dingy church and complacently endured its dinginess. Why should they fix it up? It was not their parlors; it was only a church. But Dell had about her that indescribable air which marks some people of rare good breeding, whether they chance to be clothed in calico or silk.

Mr. Nelson came hurriedly over to Dell, standing in her corner. "Are you going to stay for Sunday school, Miss Bronson?"

"Yes," she answered. It would seem a strange thing for a young lady educated by Mr. Edward Stockwell of Boston not to remain for Sunday school. This was her first Sunday at church in Lewiston. The previous Sabbath a sick headache had kept her all day a prisoner, so she was a stranger.

"Well, could you be persuaded to take our children's class? The teacher is absent, and I know of no one but you to take her place."

The children's class! That was not new work to Dell. She had been one of the teachers in the Sunday school that Uncle Edward superintended. She recalled the large, well-lighted, well-ventilated, neatly carpeted room, with its arranged rows of seats all filled with bright young faces; its teacher's desk, with its large pictorial Bible and pictorial dictionary, the silver call bell, the box of colored crayons and, at this season, a dainty vase of sweet-smelling flowers. At the right of the table stood a handsome reversible blackboard and charts. Maps of Bible lands hung all along the walls. But today she hesitated. She was not given to hesitation either. Her religious education had been "Do with thy might whatsoever thy hand findeth to do," not that later version: "Don't do anything that isn't perfectly agreeable to you in all its details, nor even then unless you feel like it."

"I am not prepared with the lesson, you know. Where is it?"

Mr. Nelson gave his shoulders an expressive shrug. "That need make no sort of difference; I fancy no one ever has prepared for that class. The lesson? Why, it's anywhere between the covers of the Bible, or out of it for that matter, if you happen to think of a story that won't hinge on a Bible verse."

Dell looked aghast. "You mean they have no regular lesson?"

"Aye. I mean just that. Each teacher revels through the realm of fact and fiction at her own sweet will, hinging her thoughts on Bible truth if she can. A wide sphere, you see, and there is always Moses in the bulrushes, you know, though I can't promise you that they may not be weary of it, as the little girl in the paper was."

"How was that?"

"Have you not seen it? Why, the story goes that the regular teacher of the class being absent, the substitute was doing Moses in the bulrushes. In the midst of her recitation one weary little five-year-old raised her hand and said: 'Oh, please, Miss Jones, I'm jest sick and tired of Moses in the bulrushes!' "

Dell laughed softly. Most of the congregation was gone now, and they were gathering for the Sunday school. Mr. Nelson perceiving this hastened his movements. "The fact is, Miss Bronson, the children's class is an experiment and is not succeeding very well because of the inefficiency of the teacher. She is never present three Sundays in succession, and sometimes I think it would be just as well if she were absent altogether. She doesn't understand the management of a young class and doesn't interest herself to learn. If you would only take it today?"

"Where is their classroom?"

"Up there."

Dell looked about her and above her but saw no chance for a classroom.

"Do you mean that hole in the wall?" she asked at last.

Mr. Nelson laughed. "Just about that. It would be a pretty fair description of the room, though there are stairs to reach it by."

"Have you a blackboard?"

"Not a bit of it. Nor a chart nor a picture — nothing but a bare room and some children."

"Without any lesson or any teacher," said Dell, her heart swelling with indignation. "Poor things! Well, I will take the class and do the best that I can for them, and I shall say nothing about Moses in the bulrushes, Mr. Nelson."

So presently he conducted her to the "hole in the wall" and left her there to do what she could. It was a long, narrow, dirty room with seats that were much too high, so that the rows of little feet dangled, and ambitious toes tried in vain to touch the floor. There were seventeen children, most of them wee ones, all staring curiously at Dell. Among them she recognized Mary, her little piqué-clad acquaintance, who was made happy and two inches taller by the gift of a special smile and bow.

"What can you sing?" was Dell's first question.

After much embarrassed fidgeting it was discovered that while one knew this piece and another that, they could not all unite on anything. They had not been in the habit of singing in the class, and they smiled at the idea as something new and funny. Their teacher immediately commenced teaching them that blessed child's hymn, "Jesus loves me, this I know; for the Bible tells me so."

After a fashion they presently sang it, and most thoroughly enjoyed doing so. Next, a lesson. But Dell soon discovered she was expected to spend the precious half-hour in hearing each child blunder through a verse of Scripture that bore not the slightest connection to any other verse recited and that probably they had repeated several times to some of their numerous teachers. Such was not Dell's idea of Sunday school teaching.

She looked about her thoughtfully. She had in mind a lesson prepared for her class in Boston, but to teach that she needed a blackboard. One of the windows had a white curtain — or one that once had been white. The other was curtainless, which suggested the idea that the fallen curtain must be somewhere. After a short search she drew it out from a pile of fallen plaster and other rubbish over in the corner. Its condition certainly could not be greatly impaired by the addition of a few pencil marks. So her resolution was swiftly taken, and in less time than it takes us to write of it the curtain was securely fastened by four pins to the wall, doing duty as a blackboard.

Meantime every eye was fixed on her in silent and wondering attention. Then she gave them this verse: "Enter not into the path of the wicked." Again and again the seventeen little tongues repeated it, until it seemed firmly fixed. Then she turned to the black-board and drew two heavy black lines starting to-gether and diverging gradually — as far apart at last as the limits of the curtain would allow. The line pointing upward was straight and firm, and the lower one was very crooked.

"Now, little folks," she said, speaking with a crisp energy that of itself would waken dormant faculties, "I'm going to tell you a story about Charlie and Johnny. They were brothers. Never mind their last name. We will call them Charlie and Johnny. What is our verse? Yes, that little boy in the corner said it just exactly right: 'Enter not into the path of the wicked.' Now this mark, that goes away down to the lower end of the curtain, I have made as a picture of the path of the wicked. You see it goes down, down, and here at the end I will put a large letter H, which will stand for the name of the place where this path ends. Who can tell me the dreadful name that we don't like to speak or think of where God said wicked people must go?"

Mary pronounced the awful word in an awe-stricken voice.

"Yes," said Dell. "That is the sad, sad word. We don't like to speak it and need not. God doesn't ask us to speak the dreadful word very often. But we must never forget that there is such a place, and that God said so. Now all the people who travel this road have a leader, someone who helps them along and who, when sometimes they want to get away, coaxes them to stay. Beside the letter H, I will put the first letter of his name: S. Who can tell me what the name is?"

The answer was given promptly.

"And now," said Dell, "let us go up here to the end

of the other line. And for the place that the line ends in, I can put another H, and all who can may tell me the name of the beautiful city where all the people who travel on this straight line will go to someday."

Every eye was fixed on the curtain that was pinned on the wall, and seventeen little tongues shouted out in chorus: "Heaven!"

"And the name of the leader? For they have a leader on the road too, and He is much greater and stronger than the other one, and He is always looking out for people who are on that crooked road down there and urging them to come up to Him. His name too starts with S, but it is so different from the other name. I will print the S right here by this H, and you may tell me the name."

And they were ready, those eager little ones, to speak the name: "Savior!"

"And now," said Dell, "for our story about Johnny and Charlie. They were — what relation were they?"

And every one of the seventeen tongues shouted "Brothers!" in a way that must have astonished the people in the church below.

"Yes, they were brothers. Every single one of you remembered; I am glad of that. They both started on their journey up here in this thick line, and for a while they kept pretty close together. They both knew about these two roads — and where they led and the two leaders. Their mother had told them all about it, and of course they thought they didn't want to travel down the crooked road with such a dreadful leader, and they almost made up their minds that they wouldn't. Boys always do. I never saw a boy or girl who really wanted to go on the crooked road. They every one almost make up their minds not to. They don't quite decide it though, for if they did they would be safe. You see, nobody can make them go on that road if they are quite determined not to.

"These two boys walked along together, very near the straight line, you see, not on it, because they were not quite decided. But they thought they were, and they meant to be very good. They said their prayers at night, and they tried to obey their mother during the day. You see how it was by this line I am drawing — they almost got on the straight road.

"One day some wicked boys asked them to run away from school, and after a while — don't you think? — they both decided to go. And then you see where they went: right down toward the crooked line as fast as they could." And with her pencil Dell turned the course of their lives downward.

"But Charlie felt very sorry that he had started, and soon he began to coax Johnny to turn back, but Johnny wouldn't. After a little while, Charlie left him and went up this way, toward the straight line. He told his mother how he had been tempted and almost gone into the wicked path, and he asked the Savior to forgive him, and he almost decided to go up into the straight path and take the Savior for his guide. But he was not quite decided yet, so he stayed below, so near, you see, that he almost touched the straight line.

"But poor Johnny! Here he was down here, on the path of the wicked. I wish I had time to tell you of all the sad things that happened to him. I'll tell you of one. Down here where I make this mark, there was a place where they sold rum, and there Johnny got in the habit of going. He bought the liquor and drank it. He began to like the taste of it very much."

Just at this point an excited little fellow in the corner called out: "Was it down to this tavern on the corner where he went?"

Poor Dell! Her own home brought forward to point her story. Her cheeks were very red, but she answered steadily: "No, that was not the place, but it was just like that place, and that tavern will do just as much harm to those coaxed into it as this one I am telling you of. Sometimes Johnny felt very sorry he had entered into this wicked path, and once or twice he made up his mind to come out of it, and he got out — here is the line to show where he went. He stopped drinking rum, and he tried to do some right things; and you see he went up toward the straight line but not into it, because he couldn't quite make up his mind to ask the Savior to lead him. If he had, he would have been safe. But the wicked people came after him, and Satan tried to get him to go back to that place and drink more rum. So one day he went down, down, right into that place again. He kept on going there and doing many wicked things, until one day when he had been drinking a great deal, they turned him out into the street. He lay in a gutter all night, and in the morning he was found dead!"

Dell's pencil and line pointed in solemn silence right at the edge of that fearful letter H. The children, awed and impressed as probably they had never been in their lives, looked and were silent.

"It was about that time," continued Dell at last, "that Charlie began to try harder than ever to get into the straight road, and yet he didn't try in quite the right way. He didn't ask the Savior to lead him. He would keep quite near the straight road for a whole day, and then he would do something wrong and go away down like this. But one day, after he was almost discouraged in trying to help himself, the

Savior kept whispering, 'Come to Me. I will help you.' After thinking it all over, Charlie quite decided to go, and that very hour he went up this way."

As Dell's pencil touched the firm straight line, little Mary, who had been growing more eager and interested every moment, suddenly broke the stillness by exclaiming, "He's in! He's in!"

The bell rang below, and Dell's half-hour was gone. She had done her best — with what result, God knew.

CHAPTER VIII

FINDING RECRUITS

"The steps of a good man are ordered by the Lord."

he cracked bell in the old church steeple clanged faithfully on that Friday evening.

Dell stood on the piazza all ready to go to the meeting with one exception. She had failed to secure the promised "one anyway," as a surety of an audience. She had tried several persons, but they all began to make excuses. As she stood leaning against the doorway, wondering if there was not another last effort she could make somewhere, a thought came to her. Sam Miller was at that moment sawing wood out in the wood yard. She could hear the lazy motion of his saw scraping back and forth. She could ask him. Of course, it was more than likely he wouldn't go, but it could do no harm to try. She ran out to him.

"Sam," she said, gathering up her dress and poising herself on an unsawn stick of wood, "I've come after you. I want you to go to the temperance meeting with me tonight. Will you?"

Sam looked first aghast, then amused.

"Why," he said, "I can't go to them sort of things. It ain't no use. It ain't of any account."

"Go and try one. I don't believe you have ever been. We are going to have singing. I know you are fond of music. I heard you singing 'Molly Bawn' this morning. I like your voice. I want you to come and help us sing."

Sam leaned on his saw meditatively.

"You'd be wanting me to sign the pledge now, I daresay, if I went there?" he said inquiringly, with a cunning look in his eyes.

"Why, of course, I should invite you to do so. Are you so afraid of a pledge that you don't even dare to meet one face-to-face for a few minutes? You won't be made to sign it, you know, if you don't choose to do so."

Sam's voice took a plaintive turn.

"It ain't no good for me to have to do with them kind of things, Miss Bronson. It ain't, truly. I'm nothing but an old loafer nowadays, and I know it, and I keep away from nice folks. I'm all gone to wreck and ruin; ain't worth taking any notice of."

Dell stooped and picked up a chip and broke it into little bits while she talked.

"You don't mean a word of that, Sam, not a single word of it. If anyone should say it to you, you would be angry enough to choke them. You know you are worth a good deal. And now and then when you look at little Mamie, you think that you'll never drink another drop of that horrid rum and that you will work hard so that Mamie can have nice things to wear and go to school and have as good a chance as any girl her age."

She had touched the tender spot in his heart. He put up his rough hand and brushed it across his eyes.

"That's true," he said at last. "True as preaching. Sometimes I think I'll manage somehow to give her a chance. But then, you see, it's no kind of use. I can't do it. I've tried and tried and made promises by the bushel, and it never did the least mite of good. I've got to drink."

There was a genuine plaintiveness in his voice this time, and Dell sensed it was time to turn comforter.

"You've never tried the help that the pledge would give you," she said cheerily. "Suppose you make a grand start and sign the pledge. That of itself will give you strength. Then temperance people will know you are trying, and we will all help you."

But Sam Miller was not to be so easily won. He really wanted to reform; that is, now and then he did, when he thought of Mamie. But the wish was very weak and wouldn't bear the test of a stern, strong effort. He turned from Dell and took his saw again with a mournful shake of the head.

"I can't do that. I know I wouldn't keep it, and where would be the use? I'd be worse off than I was before I tried."

Dell decided to waive that part of the subject.

"I have a very special reason for wanting you to go to the meeting with me tonight," she said eagerly. "You see, we each promised last week that we would bring someone with us this evening, and now if you fail me I shall have to go alone, and I don't like to at all."

Sam Miller turned halfway round again from his

stick of wood and laid down his saw. This was evidently a new phase of the question. The bright young creature before him had not been bestowing smiles and kindly words on him for nothing.

"Why, if it would be a matter of my doing you a favor," he said, speaking slowly and in much embarrassment, "why, I suppose I could go."

"It would be a real favor. I want to keep my promise, you know."

"But you won't ask me to sign one of them pledges, will you?"

"I'll ask you to, certainly, if I get a chance. But no one will compel you to sign it if you really make up your mind that you won't."

Sam meditated still further.

"Well," he said at last, "you go on, and tell 'em your someone is coming. I'll come along down that way by and by, I guess."

"Oh, no," said Dell persuasively. She was very fearful of the attractions of the barroom, which he would be likely to pass through. "That wouldn't be bringing someone with me. That's what I promised. I want you to walk down the street and into the church with me."

"Well," said Sam, giving the stick of wood an emphatic kick and speaking with decision, as if he had conquered an invisible foe. "I'll go now. I'll be hanged if I won't."

And he went. He shambled through the one long street by the side of the well-dressed young lady, and more than one lounger at the village stores looked after them with curious eyes. The bell had ceased its clanging, and there was quite a little company gathered inside the church. Much pains had been taken to spread the news of the meeting, and curiosity had drawn in several who were not deeply interested in the cause.

"There's forty-four folks in the church this very minute," Tommy Truman announced in a very loud and gleeful whisper to Dell as she entered the door.

"There are! That's splendid!" she responded in a voice not so loud but every bit as gleeful.

Then Mr. Nelson made his way toward her. "Are the lamps better?" he asked. "Haven't I improved in the art of cleaning and trimming them? Shall we open this remarkable meeting with a song, if we can get anybody to sing it?"

"A great deal brighter, Mr. Nelson. The church really looks almost cheerful. I should think it would be better to open with prayer."

The seriocomic look on Mr. Nelson's face faded into one of perplexed gravity.

"Should you?" he asked in a troubled tone.

"Why, I don't suppose it makes much difference which way it is," Dell said. "It only struck me as the most appropriate way. Would you prefer to sing first?"

"I — I had not thought it necessary to have prayer at all," he said.

It was Dell's turn to look grave and surprised.

"I confess," she said with quiet dignity, "that to me it seems almost, if not quite, a necessity."

He glanced around the room. "There is no one here to call on."

"Can't you call on yourself, Mr. Nelson?"

"Not very well; I'm not in the habit of it."

"Of praying in public do you mean?"

"Yes, or in private either," he answered her quickly, with an embarrassed laugh. "I don't wish to dress in sheep's clothing, Miss Bronson. I see you have mistaken my character."

Dell was silent from utter surprise and disappointment. But Mr. Nelson added almost immediately in a relieved tone, "Oh, we are all right after all; here comes Mr. Tresevant, and he has Miss Emmeline Elliot with him. I think she will play the organ for us, and he can pray."

While Mr. Nelson hastened to meet the minister, Dell slid quietly into a seat, still wearing her grave face. It had been a great disappointment; she had thought she had recognized one of the children of the King.

Mr. Tresevant went forward and offered a very fervent prayer. To be sure, he did not say the word *temperance*, but he slid around it and glided almost up to it in that dexterous way some good and skillful people have a habit of doing. After the prayer, a great whispering ensued. Miss Emmeline Elliot was being coaxed to play. She smiled sweetly and shook her head. She had not thought of such a thing. She had come in for a little while only as a spectator. She could not think of taking any part in the exercises. She hated to play on a cabinet organ anyway and wasn't accustomed to it, as Mr. Nelson knew, and that one was so horridly out of tune. It made her teeth ache even to hear it, and he really must excuse her.

A timid girl in the corner was petitioned. She grew red from chin to forehead at the bare thought and looked so thoroughly frightened that Mr. Nelson did not wait for the refusal. Several others were tried, with like results. Dell meantime looked on, half amused and half provoked.

"Now why can't that man ask me to play?" she said to herself. "What is the use of his taking for granted that I can't do anything? I've a mind to offer my services. I won't either. He might at least venture the inquiry. Let him go without music if he can't invite me." But as soon as she said it she chided herself for it. Uncle Edward would be proud of his pupil tonight, wouldn't he!

The end of it was that she telegraphed Tommy Truman with her eye and sent him after Mr. Nelson. He came, looking greatly perplexed, saying, "I don't see but we shall have to do without music after all."

"If you would give me an invitation, how do you know but I would play for you?" she asked.

"You?" he said, with brightening face. "Can you?"

"I can try," she answered demurely, and without further delay she walked up to the instrument. Inwardly she laughed a little at her position. It so happened that, as far as being a musician was concerned, the position was not at all novel. Even in cultured, musical Boston, her playing and voice were decidedly noticeable. And here were these people staring at her as if they could not recover from their surprise. Mr. Nelson brought her the old notebook and selected the piece he wished to sing.

"Shall I read it?" Dell questioned.

"If you can." And then her fingers swept the keys. It was a different touch from that to which the wheezy old organ was accustomed, and it rolled forth grandly in honor of its player. And when Dell's rich, full voice filled the room, the squeak and the wheezing were alike forgotten. Lewiston had a surprise. Miss Emmeline Elliot straightened herself, let her lace shawl droop gracefully or otherwise as it pleased and listened intently, discovering that she was no longer the player of Lewiston. Dell Bronson, the tavernkeeper's daughter, could draw from those disordered keys such music as she had scarcely dreamed of. The church windows and doors were wide open, and as the powerful voice rolled out, passers-by halted at the gate, listened and by twos and threes strolled in.

"Sing twenty verses, and for once in its life the church will be full," whispered Mr. Nelson in one of the interludes, as he bent with shining eyes to turn the pages. And Dell, singing on, just gloried in the power that God had given her, the power of song. Though she had sung so much, she had never realized the joy of her voice, the use to which it might be put, as she did that night.

That temperance meeting was a grand success. There was much singing (Dell was not sparing of her voice), and it fulfilled its mission well. People gathered in, so that when dainty little Mary Cobb came forward in her freshest white dress to recite her piece, she was half frightened at the rows of eyes gazing at her. She had been carefully trained, and her soft little voice was clear and sweet as she commenced that most exquisite of child poems:

> There's no rain left in the heaven!
> There's no dew left on the daisies and
>   clover,
> I've said my seven times over and over,
> Seven times one are seven.
>
> I am old, so old, I can write a letter;
> My birthday lessons are done;
> The lambs play always, they know no
>   better;
> They are only one times one.

O moon! in the night I have seen you
  sailing
And shining so bright and low;
You were bright! ah, bright! but your
  light is failing,
You are nothing now but a bow.

You moon, have you done something
  wrong in heaven
That God hath hidden your face?
I hope if you have you'll soon be for-
  given,
And shine again in your place.

O velvet bee, you're a dusty fellow,
You've powdered your legs with gold!
O brave marsh marybuds, rich and yel-
  low,
Give me your money to hold.

O columbine, open your folded wrapper,
Where two twin turtle doves dwell!
O cuckoopint, toll me the purple clapper,
That hangs in your clear green bell!
And show me your nest with the young
  ones in it;
I am old, you may trust me, linnet, linnet,
I am seven times old today.

Tommy Truman did himself and his author credit.
His round little voice rang clear and strong — and
indignantly over the wrongs and woes of a drunkard's wife. Mr. Nelson made a strong, stirring
speech, and then the singing swelled forth again.
They stood together after the meeting, Mr. Nelson,

Mr. Tresevant, Miss Elliot and Dell. Mr. Tresevant expressed himself neatly and kindly concerning the success of the meeting and the superiority of the music.

"You have really given us a delightful surprise, Miss Bronson," he said.

Miss Elliot chimed in, "Yes, indeed. I wasn't aware that you played or sang. You sing remarkably well."

Dell's eyes danced. "I wish I could have been surprised," she said, turning to Mr. Nelson. "I was in hopes that Sam Miller would surprise me by signing the pledge, but no such good fortune awaited me. Now, if I had been a heroine in a book, how promptly he would have signed the pledge and been a reformed man from this very hour, but being out of a book and in a most matter-of-fact little town, I suppose I must bide my time. By the way, Mr. Tresevant, I don't see your name here."

"No," Mr. Tresevant said, flushing slightly. "I am not a character in a book either and must therefore study my steps carefully."

CHAPTER IX

THE TEA PARTY

"I will make you fishers of men."

here'll be a high old time tonight, Miss Dell, I just expect. I don't look for nothing else." Sally volunteered this information as she cleared off the dinner table.

Dell turned from the window, where she had been overseeing some of Kate's operations, and said with a bright smile: "What kind of a time is that, Sally?"

"Why, there's a barn raising up in the hollow, and the folks will be coming home about dark, and the way they'll pour in here won't be slow, and they smokes and drinks most generally them times till twelve o'clock, and sometimes they gets pretty merry."

Dell's smile had vanished, and her eyes had an indignant flash. "I thought they had those disgraceful scenes in the barn after it was raised, and at the expense of the owner."

"So they does, the workers, but these fellows that come in here are the hangers-on, who don't do no work and can't get in at the supper, so they comes here."

The face by the window turned suddenly away from Sally, and the fair, brown head drooped low. This was bitter truth. Her father's guests were those not sufficiently respectable to be admitted to the regular merry makings — and so took refuge with him! There were times when those disgraceful truths surged over Dell with such overwhelming power that it seemed she would sink beneath them. She battled with her hot tears. They should not fall; they could do no good. She was put here for work, not for weeping. But what to do? She turned again to Sally. "Who told you about all this?"

Sally tossed her head contemptuously. "Oh, Sam Miller did. He knows everything that's a-going on, and more too. If there's a thing in Lewiston that fellow don't know about unless it's his own business, I'd like to hear what it is."

Dell left abruptly to search for Sam. He was in the barroom. For a wonder it had no other occupant. She leaned over the dirty counter.

"Sam, does Father know about the raising this afternoon?"

Sam stared. "Not as I knows on," he said at last. "No, I guess he don't. There ain't been a soul in that's spoke of it, as I've heard. He never goes, Miss Bronson." This last was in a tone intended to be encouraging.

"Well, now," said Dell in confidential tones. "I want Father all to myself this evening. Don't tell him anything about the raising. If I succeed in getting him to come with me, can't you attend to things here and not let him be called, no matter who comes? And, Sam, won't you keep things quiet out here for me?"

Sam looked at her solemnly. The poor man understood her object as plainly as though she had expressed it in words; he felt a pitiful sympathy for her struggles after her father. In a weak, childish sort of way he even thought that if she or somebody were struggling after him in that eager fashion, he would give up the rum for her sake. Meantime, of course, he forgot the struggling wife at home and little Mamie.

"I'll do it if I can," he said. "I'll do the very best I can, but I don't know how much it will be."

"I'll trust you," said Dell in earnestness, and then she vanished. Her father was in the garden hoeing. She found and followed him and promptly introduced her subject. "Father, I am going to have a tea party this afternoon. Will you come?"

"Not I," he said. "Have your tea parties and your friends, child. I'm glad to see you happy. I ain't stingy. You're welcome to all the good things you want, but don't expect me to come to 'em."

"Ah, but I do." And Dell leaned both hands on his arm in a winning fashion that reminded him of the days when Dell's young mother had clung to his arm.

"I depend on you. I have my plans all made, and you will spoil them all if you don't come. You see, there is not to be another living being there, just you and me."

Her father stared at her in a blank surprise for a few minutes. Then he leaned over his hoe and chuckled. "You're a queer fish. Now what notion will you take next, I wonder?"

"Will you come?" Dell repeated. "I am going to have just such things as you like best for supper, and I shall have the tearoom all brightened up, so much pleasanter than that long table. I never sit down with you there, you know. Will you promise?"

Mr. Bronson shook his head. "I can't, child. I've got to eat my supper with the folks. They're good enough for me, and you might sit down with us if you would. It wouldn't look right to see me away from my own table."

"Can't you be invited out to tea once in a while as well as anybody else? Father, don't you remember how you and Mother and I used to have tea together all alone, once in a while, when I was a little bit of a girl? Oh, Father, I have not had you all to myself once since I came home, and I want it so much. Won't you come?"

It is a mistake to suppose that a rumseller has no heart; they are hard to reach, it is true, and I doubt if Jonas Bronson was sure he had a heart until Dell's pleading set it into unusual motion. He looked down almost tenderly on the earnest young face.

"Well," he said at last, "it's as silly a piece of business as ever I heard of. But, land's sake, if it will do you any good, I might as well eat my supper in that room for once; so if I get back in time, I'll come."

"Oh, are you going away?" she asked with dismayed face. What if he should drop in at the raising after all?

"Got to go to the Corners this afternoon to see Jim Turner on business. I declare for it, I ought to be off this minute."

The bright look returned. "Oh, you'll get back. I

know you will. You wouldn't disappoint me for all the Jim Turners in creation. I know you won't."

It is a wonderful thing sometimes to trust a man. Perhaps after all it was more that last sentence than anything else that made Jonas Bronson actually hasten his movements and so drive up to his house ten minutes before six. Meantime Dell had not been idle. The tearoom was a marvel of freshness and beauty; there were flowers and mosses and a most daintily spread tea table. Muffins, made by Dell's own hand, such as Sally might have tried in vain to manufacture, were hot from the oven. When the work was done, Dell stood looking at it all with a pleased face. She did not expect her father to notice the flowers and mosses. Even if he did he would be likely to call them trumpery, but she had a notion the general effect of grace and beauty might linger in his memory as a pleasant thing.

She was on the watch and ran to the door at the first sound of the wheels. Presently she led her father in gleeful triumph to the tearoom and seated him in the great armchair, with a fresh newspaper in hand, while she went to her muffins. It was an odd little supper. The father and daughter sitting opposite each other at that round table had not apparently a single idea in common. The father seemed to feel it most, and it tinged his manner with embarrassment. But Dell exerted herself to talk and laugh and wait on him. And the muffins and cold chicken he certainly enjoyed, likewise the pickled lobster, sent from Boston on purpose for him.

"You're a good cook," he said as he finished his fourth cup of tea and rose from the table. "And a good girl, I guess. I reckon they ain't spoilt you in Boston, for all they tried. Anyhow, things are different about the house. You needn't think I don't notice things, 'cause I do. I know when a bed is made comfortable and when it ain't as well as the next man. Your mother was a master hand at making a bed, and you've took after her."

Dell had made her father's room over in every imaginable respect and now had it under her daily supervision. Instead of being the dingiest and most ill-kept room in the house, it had grown into one that was always fresh and cheery. This was the first time her father had by word or look evinced any knowledge of the change. It was something to know that he appreciated his bed.

She sprang up eagerly; he was looking around for his hat.

"Oh, Father, read the newspaper a few minutes while I get rid of this table, and then I have something to show you. Here is a Boston daily, which came just a few minutes ago."

"I don't know about it," he said doubtfully. "Guess I ought to go." Nevertheless he took the paper and sat down, while Dell almost breathlessly hurried the dishes out to Kate.

Every nerve was on the alert. There was a drawn battle between the tearoom and the barroom that evening, and the daughter knew only too well what a powerful ally that barroom possessed. She came in with a small square board filled with pegs. Watching for her chance as he began to turn the paper restlessly, she produced it.

"Father, are you as sharp at puzzles as you used to be? Do you remember those you used to get out for Mother? Here is one I have looked at a great many times, and I don't get it at all."

"Oh, I don't fuss at such nonsense now," he said.

"I used to amuse your mother in that way once in a while; you remember it, do you? Hmm, you was just a little mite of a child."

"I wish you would help me with this," Dell said, bending over it with a perplexed face. "I can't see through this in the least, and it provokes me to fail in anything."

The father chuckled admiringly. "It does, eh? You're a chip off the old block. I've seen the time that I've bothered for hours over the things, and I always beat 'em too. Let's see this one."

Never was the game of solitaire so closely and eagerly watched. Dell bent over the board with shining eyes, having in her heart the eager hope not that he would succeed, but that he would fail again and again — for this once accomplished, what could she do next? There seemed little fear of its being accomplished; apparently he had found something that would beat him. He knitted his brows and pulled out the pegs and studied them in every imaginable way and finally threw the puzzle down with an impatient "Pshaw! The thing is a humbug. There can't nobody do it."

"Professor Thompson can do it in a twinkling," Dell said. "I've seen him, but he does it so fast you can't tell anything about it. Uncle Edward and I have sat and looked right at him and then tried, and we couldn't get it."

"Your Uncle Edward can't get it, eh — with all his book learning?" He drew it toward him again. The wrinkles came in his forehead, and he was again absorbed.

Dell looked about her for a fan and fanned hard and fast. She had been so frightened lest the puzzle had failed her. There came a low tap at the side door.

Dell rose and opened it softly. It was Sally, respectful and sympathetic, perfectly comprehending what her young mistress was about. She spoke in whispers. "Mr. Elliot and Mr. Nelson are waiting in the parlor to see you, Miss Dell."

Dell did not hesitate for an instant. "Tell them I am very much engaged, and they must excuse me this evening. And, Sally, if anyone else should call, just excuse me without coming."

Slowly but surely the evening waned, and still the puzzle held sway. They had conversation over it now and then. Her father called it the confoundest thing that had ever got hold of him. He slammed it down on the table several times, and as often some remark of Dell's about Uncle Edward's trials over it would give him a fresh impulse. Suddenly a prolonged and triumphant "Aha!" announced a victory. Dell had accomplished the feat. But even then Dell had to be taught, and she proved a stupid pupil, and when she finally felt that it would be wise to learn, her father immediately said: "There! You've got it. Now I must go. I don't know what that Sam may be about. That lobster of yours must have been uncommon salty. I'm as dry as a fish."

Dell sprang up. "Oh, are you? How glad I am. I have been hoping you would say so. Now I'm going to give you a splendid surprise. You think, I suppose, that Sally knows how to make coffee, but you wait just a minute and see what you think of mine."

There was a low call to Sally, who seemed to be in waiting. A few hurried words with her, and in moments her father was drinking a cup of very strong, very richly sugared, very thickly creamed coffee — precisely what he liked.

"It is good, that's a fact," he said as he poured it

down. The little coffee pot was on hand, and Dell hastened to replenish his cup.

As she gave it to him she asked: "Do you like singing as much as you used to, Father? You have not heard me since I came home. I know that old ballad that Mother used to sing. I'm going to sing it for you."

And immediately her full, rich voice filled the room. Her father drank his coffee more slowly and presently set down his cup, got out his handkerchief and blew his nose. More memories were woven around that song than his daughter knew of. He said not a word when it was finished. Indeed, she hardly gave him a chance but warbled off into another old song. Song after song was finished and another commenced, and still he sat silent and attentive, until his head began to droop. He gave several emphatic nods and finally settled back against the wall and snored. Dell sang on softly, not daring to stop at first. But soon the snoring became so well-defined that she ceased her music. Still she stirred neither hand nor foot. If this blind nap would only wear out the rest of the evening! And so, silent and motionless, she sat through her vigil. The clock from the distant kitchen struck faintly. She tried to count. Could it be possible it was ten o'clock? She drew her tiny watch. Yes. Victory! The evening was gone.

With a reassuring look at the sleeper, Dell stole softly from the room, across the dining room and hall, and peeped into the barroom from the half-open door. It was unusually quiet. A few loungers lingered in various stages of drunkenness and sleep. The half-filled, badly trimmed lamps cast their smoky light over the miserable scene. With no intention to make the barroom inviting, Dell left it to uninterrupted dirt and gloom.

Sam Miller caught a glimpse of her and came out, speaking earnestly. "I've kept things just as still as I could. There came a lot of fellows about an hour ago. They made a great row and wanted to see your father, but I told them he was out to tea and could not be seen, and pretty soon they went off."

Dell looked at him gratefully. "I know you have kept it very still, and I thank you. Now, Sam, can't you have these people go away? And put out the lights? It's time, I'm sure, and I don't want Father to come here tonight."

"Yes," Sam said virtuously. "It is time, that's a fact. And, yes, I can manage that for you. I'll send them home." Which he did most unceremoniously. "Here, you, Dick Johnson, go and sleep on your own floor. You can't have ours any longer. Jim Cole, get up and go home." And in less than fifteen minutes each sleepy loafer had staggered off, and the lights were out.

Dell went back to the tearoom, satisfied that her father could awaken now whenever he chose. In a few minutes a more decided snore than usual roused him. He looked around with a bewildered air and remarked that he guessed he had been asleep. He yawned and stretched himself and, drawing his great watch, said: "Well, I swan! If it ain't going on to eleven o'clock! Why, what the dickens has been going on in the barroom, I wonder."

"It's all right, Father," Dell said. "Sam has closed things up and gone home. I told him you were tired, and I thought you wouldn't be out."

"The mischief," he said, staring. "This is a funny evening, I declare. Well, I am tired, that's a fact. Give me another drink of your coffee, and I'll go to bed."

The door closed on him at last, and Dell sat down on the couch with a weary sigh. A funny evening! Well, it had certainly been a strange one. How hard she had worked, and after all what had she accomplished? It was only one evening. She felt like a feather trying to beat back the ocean waves. Would she ever be able to stem the awful tide that was setting against her?

She drew the large Bible to her, the one she had placed conspicuously on the little table. Turning the leaves, she paused over the story of the weary fishermen who had toiled all night and taken nothing. She read the story through, gleaning courage. "Nevertheless at thy command, we will let down the net." There was another verse, "Follow me, and I will make you fishers of men."

Was not the message to her? Fishers of men. Wasn't she willing to do the work? What if she did toil all night and take nothing? Nevertheless at His command. Who could tell what the fruits of this one evening might be? Couldn't God use her toiling? Wasn't it something to have charmed her father into a quiet evening instead of leaving him to a drunken revel? Yes, she would toil not only all night but many nights. Wasn't there always before her the promise "I will make you fishers of men"? With this to plead — the elder Brother's own words — could she ever weary over the toiling?

CHAPTER X

DELL'S VISITORS

*"I know thy works,
that thou art neither cold nor hot."*

r. Chester Elliot and the Reverend Mr. Carroll Tresevant selected the same evening in which to call on Dell. It was not by any means Mr. Elliot's first call. Anxious to atone for the neglect of his sister, he had been very cordial and courteous in his attentions. Nor was it the first visit for the young minister.

This evening's conversation on general topics had been decidedly enjoyable until a slight pause when Dell suddenly turned to Mr. Elliot: "By the way, we are in need of your assistance, Mr. Elliot. Why don't you join our temperance society?"

He laughed good-humoredly. "I am afraid you wouldn't admit me."

"We certainly would, and we'd be glad to do so.

We only ask you to sign the abstinence pledge — that constitutes membership."

"Whether it is kept or not, Miss Bronson?" said Mr. Tresevant.

Something peculiar in the minister's manner annoyed Dell, and she answered, with a heightened color, "Of course we believe our members sign in good faith, with intent to keep their promises."

"Which, nevertheless, and unfortunately, they sometimes fail to do. What then?"

"Then happens just what happens in other matters where people fail to keep their promises: They lower themselves in their own estimation and in that of others."

"And do you consider a man better or worse because of a broken pledge?"

Dell's eyes flashed. "Do you consider a man better or worse who pledges himself to Christ and then, as unfortunately many do, breaks his pledge?"

"Worse, decidedly," Mr. Tresevant said.

"Do you therefore try to deter a man from uniting with Christ lest he may sometime in the future break his promises?" she pressed.

Mr. Tresevant fidgeted a little in his chair and toyed with the top of his cane. "I do not, of course," he said at last. "But I need not remind you, Miss Bronson, that the cases are not parallel. When a person desires to unite with the church, we trust he leans upon the divine arm for strength, and there is therefore little danger of his falling. But in the matter of a total abstinence pledge, it is merely a compact between man and his own weak will."

"I didn't know it," Dell answered gravely. "I supposed that every attempt on our part to do right was an evidence of the guiding of the divine arm. I imagined that our own weak wills, left to themselves, did not so much as conceive of a right desire."

Mr. Elliot turned with a half-amused, half-earnest air toward his pastor: "That is the theology you preach, is it not, sir?"

"In general terms, yes," Mr. Tresevant said, "but Miss Bronson has very naturally confused the two points."

"I don't in the least understand what you mean," Dell said. "But I seem to have a higher opinion than you of our weak human wills. If Mr. Elliot should promise to pay me a certain sum of money on a certain day and should sign a note to that effect, I must say I should be inclined to think he would do it. Now I didn't mean to open a discussion on temperance, only to ask why he didn't join our society."

"I thought we had thrown you off your track," said Mr. Elliot gaily. "And, behold, here you are at the very same station. Well, the truth is, if I must confess it, I don't think I am prepared to keep the pledge. I should have no objections to signing it if I thought it at all probable that I should keep it for twenty-four hours."

"I am sorry you have so little confidence in your own strength of purpose," Dell said dryly.

"No, you mistake. It is not strength of purpose that is needed, but inclination. You see, I have never been converted to the necessity of total abstinence."

"Oh," Dell said. "If you had the misfortune to live where I do, you would be a speedy convert, I fancy. And I suspect that one day spent at your father's factory would be likely to have the same effect."

"That is just the point on which we should differ. If you crusaders would confine your efforts to the lower classes, I should be with you heartily. I think you might do a vast deal of good. But I cannot see the use of fettering the world because a few poor wretches abuse their privileges."

Dell's lip curled just a little, and she spoke rapidly: "Do you believe what you are saying, Mr. Elliot? Suppose you talk your theory to Pat Hughes, for instance? I believe he is one of your father's men. Tell him liquor is a very improper article for him to use — that he belongs to the lower classes and therefore cannot control his appetite; that he ought by all means to sign the pledge. But that you, being made of different dust from him, shall continue the moderate use of liquor. How long would you talk before seeing him a reformed man?"

Mr. Elliot shrugged his handsome shoulders. "I shall expect the millennium to come before even you can reform poor Pat. But I don't have to carry Pat's conscience, you know. It is enough for me to look after my own."

"Oh, the old argument 'Am I my brother's keeper?' As a Christian you are bound to make every effort to give up every indulgence that might stand in his way. By so doing you might save one soul, made even of such common clay as Pat Hughes."

The flush on Mr. Elliot's cheek deepened slightly, but he answered courteously and with a strong attempt at playfulness: "You are rather hard on me, Miss Bronson, to lay Pat's failings at my door. He was a drunkard before I was born. You challenge me, but I don't think I stand alone in the matter. Here is Mr. Tresevant. You will admit that he views things from a Christian standpoint. Now if you can prevail on him to sign the pledge, I will put my name under his."

Mr. Tresevant looked annoyed. He hadn't expected to be backed into a corner this way.

"Miss Bronson and I should differ as to the ways and means, rather than as to the sin of drunkenness," he said quietly. "Of course, if I were convinced of the total abstinence pledge's being the best way of meeting this important question, I would sign it without hesitation."

"Perhaps I don't think it the best way myself," Dell answered promptly. "But since it is one of the best ways we have at present, why not use it as far as it goes?"

"But you don't approve of total abstinence pledges at all, do you, sir?" said Mr. Elliot. "I have heard so at least."

"To abstain from the use of liquor, a man doesn't have to write his name on a bit of paper."

"But the pledge has repeatedly proven itself a help to people," Dell replied.

"There have been instances undoubtedly wherein men considered themselves helped by the pledge, and we are bound to believe them."

"Why not promote its circulation? It certainly can do no injury."

"All are not agreed on that point, you know." Mr. Tresevant's reply was very kind and given with a smile.

As a matter of fact, Dell did not know it; at least she did not know that Christians differed.

She spoke in a dismayed tone: "Do *you* think it does injury, Mr. Tresevant?"

"I think there are natures that it might injure. I should hesitate to press a pledge of that nature upon persons."

"Will you be kind enough to tell me why?"

"I am not sure I can do so briefly. For one thing,

you are aware, of course, that many persons, maybe most persons, are impelled to do that which they have promised not to do. I have no doubt that the pledge can create, or at least stimulate, the desire."

Dell surveyed him in unaffected amazement, and her voice had almost a touch of scorn: "Is it then only the total abstinence pledge that works in this manner, or do you think that the command 'Thou shalt not steal' is the author of all the dishonesty in the world?"

Mr. Tresevant laughed. "You are a casuist, Miss Bronson, are you not?" he asked, with unfailing courtesy.

"But," said Dell, "I don't understand. I am sure we do not consider other promises as having such disastrous results. Church pledges, bank pledges, marriage vows, the whole long list of promises, given and received daily, in the social and business world — nobody seems to have conscientious scruples against them?"

"There is scarcely such a drawing away toward the breaking of any of these as there often is in the case of the total abstinence pledge."

"But is the boy who promises his mother never to touch wine, who when pressed by evil companions to drink answers nobly, 'I cannot; I promised Mother I wouldn't,' really weakened, injured by his promise?"

"Well," said Mr. Tresevant, again smiling, "that is putting the case somewhat strongly perhaps. I would not be understood to be out of sympathy with the temperance reform. Intemperance is a gigantic evil, and it is right to combat it; but people must be allowed to choose their own weapons and to think less of some than of others."

"What weapon would you recommend in the place of the temperance pledge?" Dell pressed.

"The great weapon to be used above all others against the sin and suffering in this world is the religion of Jesus Christ," answered Mr. Tresevant with the satisfaction of one who thinks he has made an unanswerable remark. But the answer, or rather the next question, was quick and pointed.

"Then you consider that a man who has been persuaded to sign a total abstinence pledge is a less hopeful subject of divine grace than a drunkard?"

What answer the minister of the gospel would have made to this very singular question cannot be known. Mr. Elliot came to the rescue.

"But surely total abstinence and temperance are two different subjects. Aren't you confusing them, Miss Bronson?"

"I hardly call them distinct subjects, Mr. Elliot, and, therefore, of course, cannot confuse them."

Mr. Elliot looked annoyed. "But you certainly do not think that every man who occasionally drinks a glass of wine or even of hard cider is going to become a drunkard? I see your pledge prohibits even cider."

"I think that I cannot possibly tell unless I meet him ten or twenty years from now. But this I know, that every poor drunkard on earth began by drinking only an occasional glass. Men do not plunge into drunkenness as they do into the river to commit suicide. And I sincerely believe the Christian standpoint to be 'Look not upon it!' The law of expediency ought to prove that, even to those who have no fears for themselves."

"But, Miss Bronson, you involve yourself in logical difficulties, do you not, when you take such ground?" It was the soft, calm voice of the minister.

"For instance, there are people in this world who just as certainly kill themselves from overeating, as others do from overdrinking. Should you then, as a Christian woman, abstain from the use of food?"

"Yes," said Dell, her eyes snapping. "Just as soon as I discover that a large proportion of my brothers and sisters are ruining their bodies and wrecking their souls, not only for time but for eternity, and bringing absolute ruin on their families from overeating; and as soon as I discover that I am setting them an example, when food is not only not a necessity of life at all, nor even conducive to health, but is on the contrary considered by eminent men a positive injury — just so soon will I consider it my duty to abstain from the use of food."

At this point, with a good deal of bang and scuffle, Mr. Bronson appeared on the scene. Mr. Tresevant immediately stood and extended his hand. Mr. Elliot followed his example, and Dell brought forward a chair, which she had no sooner done than she was sorry for it. Her father's unusually talkative mood proved to her that he had been taking much more than his usual amount of liquor. And when he called her abruptly to account for not treating her friends and, opening the hall door, yelled to Sam to bring the best brandy there was in the bar, her misery was at its height. Talking on loud and fast until Sam appeared, the host took the salver and approached the clergyman.

"What! No brandy?" he said in apparent surprise as Mr. Tresevant refused. "Oh, well, you're a parson. We must excuse you, I suppose, though I've heard say you was a good hand at cider, and I'll be hanged if I haven't seen a man get drunker than a fool on cider. Well, my hearty, you and I will have a drink together, anyhow. We ain't parsons."

Mr. Elliot, being divided between his desire not to anger the drunken man and not to offend Dell, stood irresolute. Not so Dell. She came around to her father's side, laid her hand on his shoulder and said in gentle yet firm tones: "Father, I consider that any guest of mine who drinks liquor in my presence has insulted me."

"That being the case," said Mr. Elliot, "I am sure Mr. Bronson will excuse me." Immediately both gentlemen arose to depart, as Mr. Bronson, staring and muttering ominously, backed out of the room, his refreshment in hand.

Standing before them, a ghastly pale Dell spoke in low, cold tones, but her voice trembled, betraying a deeper emotion: "I trust you gentlemen will be prepared to excuse my extreme total abstinence principles. There was a time not many years ago when my father took only an occasional glass of hard cider."

CHAPTER XI

How to Teach Reckless Boys

*"I came not to call the righteous,
but sinners to repentance."*

hey are a very wild set," said Mr. Nelson. "In fact, I am not sure there are five wilder young men in the factory."

"That is encouraging!" Dell said.

"Well, in one sense it is. At least it is very astonishing that they are willing to come to Sunday school even once more."

"Have they been before?"

"Oh, yes, several times. Never for two Sundays in succession. Once they left in the midst of the exercises, and once they got into such uproarious laughter that the teacher left them in a huff or a fright, I hardly know which. It was unfortunate anyway, for since that time their aim has been to dispose of every teacher given them. I think that is their principal object in being willing to try Sunday school again."

107

"And you want me to try to teach such a class?" Dell said.

"That is precisely what I want," he answered, laughing. "You see, Miss Bronson, it resolves itself into this," he spoke seriously now. "There is absolutely no one else, not a single person, who is willing to make the attempt. I have asked Mr. Tresevant, but he assures me he cannot. I think he is not disposed to risk the chances; they would be more than likely to make sport of everything he said, and I fancy he does not like to compromise his dignity. Perhaps he is right. Besides, as you well know, he teaches a class of good Christian young ladies, including Miss Emmeline Elliot. Save you, it is next to impossible to beg a teacher from his class — they are so attached to their teacher."

"Mr. Nelson," said Dell, who had been thinking her own thoughts during the time, "what do you honestly suppose I could do with such a class as you describe?"

"That I honestly don't know," he said, laughing again. "I am extremely anxious to try you, and so discover. More truthfully, I really don't expect you to do much of anything with them. I don't think anyone can. But I want to avoid the necessity of saying, 'Boys, you may come to the Sunday school, of course, but we haven't a man or woman in our church who dares to undertake the charge of you, therefore you must be teacherless.' That is about what they expect, and they delight in the thought. Now I did not come to you having any hope that you would grant my request. But, as I told you before, you are my last resort. And if these fellows are willing to come inside the church, if only for one Sabbath, isn't it a pity to lose the chance of saying something that might possibly do them good?"

"Mr. Nelson, you are the strangest man I ever met."

Mr. Nelson, turned suddenly from the subject that engrossed his thoughts, raised his eyebrows. "I am? That amazes me. I thought I was very commonplace. May I inquire your meaning?"

"Why, your conversation would lead me to suppose that your life was permeated with a high Christian principle. Yet you disclaim all title to the name Christian. I do not understand it."

"I think I may say that I am actuated by principle," he said, smiling gravely. "The principle of love to the whole human race."

"Then I cannot see how you can help owning allegiance to Him who so loved the whole human race that He not only died for it but lived for it solely, on this weary earth, for thirty-three years!" said Dell.

Her companion was entirely grave now — and apparently sad. After a little silence he said, " 'By their fruits ye shall know them.' That is a Bible doctrine, is it not? I shall have to confess to you that the fruits that have fallen under my knowledge have not been such as to lead me to admire the tree on which they grew."

"Have you no exceptions to make?"

"Oh, yes, indeed, I would not have you think me so cynical. Yes, I have known noble Christian men and women and admired them, but, pardon me, they really seemed to be the exceptions."

There stood on the table beside Dell a neglected dish of fruit. All the good apples had been culled, leaving only the gnarled ones. She picked up a small, worm-eaten one that was beginning to decay. Holding it by the stem, she said, "Ought you to judge the fruit of the apple tree by this specimen?"

He looked at the apple, then at her. Smiling, he bowed slightly and said: "I accept your rebuke. But, Miss Bronson, what about my boys? Are they doomed to go teacherless?"

"Why don't you take them yourself, Mr. Nelson?"

"There are two reasons: In the first place, I have a class that I gathered at infinite pains. They have never had another teacher, and no other stands ready to take them. Second, now I shall run the risk of appearing inconsistent again, but I do feel the need of securing for them a teacher who knows experientially about this high Christian principle of which you speak."

Dell was silent and thoughtful. A verse of Scripture sounded through her brain: "Whatsoever thy hand findeth to do," and yet another, "Whatsoever he saith unto you, do it."

"What do you mean by their being a wild set?" she asked suddenly. "How wild are they?"

"Oh, they swear outrageously and smoke profusely and gamble whenever they get a chance, not often for money, for they have little, but for raisins or pins or straws or anything that is convenient. And they use liquor freely, every one of them."

"Mr. Nelson," said Dell, "I'm afraid I should fail miserably with such a class, and wouldn't that be worse for them than if I had not tried?"

"They have had no other teaching than continued failures. They never had the same teacher twice, as no one would attempt it a second time, although we have managed to be very unfortunate in our selections. One began at once to talk to them personally about their wicked ways. Another addressed them solemnly as 'my dear young friends.' You see, you start with at least equal hopes of success. Besides, what do you Christian people believe in regard to these matters? Have I not heard something about not leaning on the arm of flesh?"

A little silence fell between them, but at last Dell broke it. "Well, Mr. Nelson, I will do the very best I can."

Thus it came to pass that Dell Bronson, daintily clothed in purest white, stood in the doorway of the old church on the next Sabbath morning, waiting for Mr. Nelson to show her to her class.

"Are they here?" she asked as he came toward her.

"Every one of them, excessively amused over his own wit and ready for almost anything. So am I. I shall not be surprised in the least to be called on to help quell a riot. I don't know what turn their fun will take."

"I don't know whether I can do anything with them or not, but I am going to try," Dell answered. "Mr. Nelson, I want their names on a card. Do they know I am their teacher?"

Mr. Nelson shook his head. "I speculated some little time as to whether I would inform them. I finally decided not to. I didn't like to risk it. Here are the names. Shall I go in and give you a formal introduction?"

Dell took the card and studied it carefully. "Jack Cooley, Jim Forbes, John Barney, Dick Holmes, Henry Day. Do you suppose I shall ever know more about them personally than I do today?"

Mr. Nelson shook his head. "I will neither encourage nor discourage you. I am in as noncommittal a state of mind as can be imagined."

"That is remarkable encouragement," Dell said, smiling. "No, thank you, I will introduce myself."

Then she went in and took a seat in front of the five boys. They looked at her and at each other, chuckled and whistled not very loud and made observations about her under their breath. The moment the opening exercises were concluded, she turned toward them with a very cheery "Good morning, young gentlemen. I don't know but you have the advantage of me. I presume you know that I am Miss Bronson, while I know your names, it is true, but haven't an idea which name belongs to which person. I shall have to ask your help. Will you be kind enough to tell me which is Mr. Cooley?"

If Dell had only known it, she had taken them at a disadvantage. They had been taught, or at least talked at, by middle-aged gentlemen in spectacles, by middle-aged ladies with severely rebuking faces, people who had evinced more or less embarrassment or bewilderment, as if they had said: How shall we approach these young savages? But the boys had never in their lives come in contact with a young, pretty, exquisitely dressed lady, who surveyed them with utmost composure, without a trace of bewilderment or embarrassment, who addressed them with courteous politeness, as became a young lady speaking to young gentlemen. Not a single one of them laughed as they had previously expected to do. And the corner one answered promptly, "My name's Cooley."

"Well, then, Mr. Cooley," Dell said, holding out her hand and smiling, "will you introduce me to the rest of your friends?"

Which Mr. Cooley, much to his own amazement, found himself doing, in a fashion somewhat unlike ordinary introductions to be sure, but it answered Dell's purpose very well. After a few minutes' preliminary talk, she suddenly asked a question that seemed to astonish them greatly: "Are you interested in the lesson for today?"

It had never before occurred to any of the teachers that the young men could be interested in any lesson. They stared at each other and laughed a little. Finally Mr. Cooley ventured to remark: "We ain't no kind of an idea where the lesson is."

"Oh, you have not studied it then?" the teacher said, speaking as if that were a surprise. "Then of course you will not be particularly interested in it. I find it a lesson that requires a great deal of study. I have spent about four hours on it this week."

At which remark Jim Forbes was very much amazed. "For the land's sake!" he said. "How many verses is there in it?"

And upon being informed that there were only seven, he said with a contemptuous air that he would bet a goose he could learn them seven verses in a good deal less than four hours.

"Oh, it wasn't the committing to memory that took so long," Dell explained; "but there was so much to think about in it all. It is about the blind man, you know, who sat by the wayside begging. He called to Jesus, you remember, as soon as he heard He was passing by and begged for his sight to be restored. Jesus heard his call and gave him his sight. I spent a good deal of time in trying to find out why the story was put in the Bible, and how many similar points there are between this blind man and the people around us who are blind. Well, the more I thought about it, the more interested I became."

"Did you find out what they put it in the Bible for?" Dick Holmes asked.

"Why, yes," said Dell. "I think I found some reasons: Reading of wonderful cures gives you confidence in a physician, you know. Then it interested me that the blind man seemed wholly conscious of his own state. He knew he was blind."

"I don't think that's anything great," Jim Forbes said. "I should think a fellow might find out mighty quick whether he was blind or not."

"I don't know. I was thinking he might have argued something like this: 'I don't believe I'm blind. People make a great fuss about seeing. I don't think it amounts to much. I shouldn't wonder if I can see as well as anybody can. What is seeing, anyway? Very likely there is no such thing!' Haven't you heard people argue something in that way about things of which they know nothing?"

Jack Cooley laughed. He had, he said, but Dick Holmes was ready for an argument. "Yes, but you can prove to a blind man that he can't see, because you can describe things to him that he knows he never saw."

"But how are you going to make him believe you have seen them? Can't I, being a Christian, describe things to a person that he knows he has never felt, and won't he be very likely to say, 'That's all imagination on her part; I don't believe a word of it'?"

Then several of the others laughed and looked curiously at Dick, because this was precisely what he was in the habit of saying. Their looks made him reckless, and he spoke with an air of defiance: "Well, I don't. I don't believe anything. I think these Bible stories are all humbug. I don't believe there ever was any blind man who got his sight again in the way it tells about. I think religion is all a pack of lies!"

Then he folded his arms and sat back triumphantly and waited for the shocked look that he delighted to bring to people's faces. But he looked in vain; Dell's face was as serene as a summer morning.

"Yes," she said, as if she might perhaps agree with every word he said. "But, Mr. Holmes, you said you didn't believe anything. Of course, you didn't quite mean that. Don't you believe, for instance, that people die?"

Mr. Holmes admitted that he did.

"You really have no doubt about it, have you, but that all the people in this world will die?"

No, he hadn't the least doubt about that.

"Well now, my Bible states that fact distinctly — stated it hundreds of years ago — not only that everybody would die, but what would be about the average length of life. Now just suppose, for argument's sake, that everything else the Bible states should happen to be true as well? There are certain things that in one sense we cannot prove until we die. But since we know that we have to die, wouldn't it be wise to be on the safe side — to have the chance of securing all the joy of which the Bible speaks, if there should be any such thing to secure?"

It was a strange way of putting the question — a new way to them. They looked at each other in puzzled silence. Yes, the thought interested them, and Dell had very little difficulty keeping up the interest to the end. The superintendent's bell rang while they were still sitting thoughtful and quiet, boldly discussing questions that no one had ever before permitted them to broach.

"Did you give them a morphine powder?" Mr. Nelson asked as he met Dell in the hall. "I certainly never knew them to be quiet before."

"Mr. Nelson," she said, "they every one promised me they would come next Sunday."

CHAPTER XII

THE TEMPERANCE DIALOGUE

Vow, and pay unto the Lord your God.

ell had been very busy for two weeks. Mr. Nelson's last brilliant idea had occupied all her leisure time. It was complete now in all its details. The girls were perfect in their parts, and the eventful evening had arrived. They were to have another temperance meeting, the distinguished feature of which was to be an original colloquy, "The Pledge," performed by members of the society.

The author of the script had not been announced. Only Dell and Mr. Nelson knew. To show you how well the new idea succeeded, I will recount the whole performance. First was the reading of the pledge by Mr. Nelson:

"I hereby solemnly promise to abstain from the use or sale of all spirituous or malt liquors, wine or

117

hard cider as a beverage."

Then Tommy Truman had a word:

"Is there a father or mother who loves his or her children who would not be glad to have the names of those children on this pledge? Is there a sister, a child, a wife, a Sunday school teacher, who would not rejoice over the added names of their dear ones? Can there be any good reason for refusing to sign the pledge? Can there be two sides to this question? Are we not all agreed?"

His sturdy little friend and fellow-signer, Harry Mason, made the somewhat pompous answer: "There are undoubtedly two sides to this question. Many persons differ — and may we not say differ honestly? — from the views that have been expressed. They would like to be heard before being condemned. Are there not thousands of people, good people too, who never touch the accursed thing, and yet sign no pledge?"

Tommy Truman responded: "Is that an argument, my friend? I can't see how your thousands would be worse off if they proclaimed their temperance principles by signing the pledge and thus helped others to know where they stood."

Harry answered with indignant eyes and puffy cheeks: "But can't you trust a man when he promises you, without putting that promise on paper?"

Tom Stuart was on hand next. "Our friend forgets that we don't ask his name on the pledge because we do not trust him without it, but to help him to trust himself. Every honest man knows that his determination to do or not to do a thing grows stronger and firmer every time he commits himself in words or on paper. Every true man honors his promise, and, if he means it, he is not ashamed to confirm his own resolution by putting his name to it."

Then Harry, contemptuously: "Let the weak ones sign it then. We who are strong and have principle need no pledge."

Mr. Nelson's kind, grave voice made answer: " 'We then that are strong are to bear the infirmities of the weak, and not to please ourselves.' "

There was a Mary Truman, who now took up the question: "But suppose we sign the pledge and break it. Would not that be a great sin? Is it not better to drink wine a hundred times than to break one promise?"

Tommy's answer burst forth: "I say, sign to keep and not to break. 'No drunkard shall inherit the kingdom of heaven,' my Bible says. If you are afraid you will break the pledge, then you are in danger already, and who more than you needs the restraining power of a sacred pledge? Afraid you may break it and go back? Why, you are back now. You are the very one who needs help, and if you have any regard for your word, the pledge will help you."

Will Jones was the next speaker: "I have no desire to make a display of my temperance principles. How many people sign the pledge because they would have people think them very good and self-denying? I have seen enough of this empty pretense, this temperance hypocrisy, whereby people drink on the sly and yet get a name for abstinence. 'Let not your left hand know what your right hand doeth.' "

Susy Carter answered him: "That's the strangest argument I have ever heard yet. I won't write any letters to my friends, for that would be making a parade of my affections. There are people in this world who cheat; therefore, I won't profess not to. Then the idea of quoting from the Bible to match that style of argument! It must be the only verse that gentleman knows. He cannot, at least, have come across this one: 'By their fruits you shall know them'; or, 'Neither do men light a candle and put it under a bushel, but on a candlestick, and it giveth light unto all that are in the house'; or this, 'Let your light so shine before men, that they may see your good works and glorify your Father which is in heaven.' "

A nice elderly lady, deeply interested in the cause, had been coaxed into service. She now popped up and spoke earnestly: "For my part, I don't see no great difference between drinking brandy and wine and eating it. So long as you folks like mince pies and nice sauce as well as you do, you hadn't ought to come down on them that makes them for you."

Her own grandson, a splendid young fellow, answered her: "I agree with you. It is as well to drink as to eat brandy. But, Grandma, can't you make mince pies without brandy? And is there no other delicious sauce but this? Are we indeed as badly off about our food as was Miss Flora McFlimsey about her finery? She had forty dresses yet nothing to wear. Our heavenly Father has filled the world full of good things, and yet without mince pies mixed with brandy we are in danger of starvation!"

Miss Lilly Archer asked the next question: "May I ask abstainers if any such pledge as the one given here this evening can be found in our Bible? The very last chapter warns against adding anything to this sacred book. Will not those abstainers be cursed for being wise above what is written? Before I sign this pledge, I must have a 'Thus saith the Lord.' "

Tommy Truman was ready with an answer: " 'But they said, We will drink no wine: for Jonadab the son of Rechab our father commanded us, saying, Ye shall drink no wine, neither ye nor your sons for ever.... Thus have we obeyed the voice of Jonadab the son of Rechab our father in all that he hath charged us, to drink no wine all our days, we, our wives, our sons, nor our daughters.' That's the Bible! Jeremiah 35. Doesn't it sound somewhat like a pledge? Perhaps you would like also to hear something about the Nazarites' temperance pledge — and Daniel's and Jeremiah's and Paul's."

Then Fred Edson had a word to say: "But did not Noah drink freely, and wasn't he a good man? Did not the priests and kings of Judah? Did not Jesus? They called Him a wine-bibber. And were not the disciples in the habit of drinking all they wished? Peter, in his great Pentecostal sermon, does not deny that his friends were fond of wine; he merely says they were not drunk so early in the morning. At the communion table did not the Savior command them to drink the wine? 'Drink ye all of it.' Then remember what Paul tells young Timothy: 'Take a little wine for thy stomach's sake.' What can you say to that?"

Tommy Truman was ready for him: "I can say — are you Timothy? Have you Timothy's complaint? Has Paul examined your physical disorder and directed wine; and have you some of Timothy's wine? 'Noah drank freely,' you say. Yes, and got drunk; therefore we must. Solomon had many wives; must we? David committed murder. Peter swore. You say Christ commanded them to drink wine. He even changed water into wine. But what if that wine made at the marriage in Cana and that made at the communion and that recommended by Paul to Timothy was all new, the fresh juice of the grape? Then where is your Bible for touching the filthy, poisoning stuff sold in barrooms and saloons?"

Then young Williams: "Oh, do stop this talk about poison. Doesn't the Bible say, 'Every creature of God is good, and nothing to be refused'? Isn't wine a good creature of God? Has the Creator taken so much pains to make all these things, and shall we call them nasty poisons? Let's beware how we pour contempt on the Word of God and on His good creatures."

This brought Edward Phillips to his feet with glowing face: "Every creature of God is good. Good to eat and drink you mean? Rattlesnakes are creatures; so are crows. Would you like a dish of them to eat? How about poison ivy, quicksilver and nitric acid? If we do not drink every liquid, we pour contempt upon the Bible. Is that the argument?"

Fred Edson, meantime, seemed to have thought of a new idea: "But are we not called unto liberty, while this pledge of yours makes one a slave? Did not our forefathers bleed and die to eat and drink what they would? Have you never seen the Declaration of Independence and its list of glorious signers? Have you never heard 'Give me liberty or give me death'? Shall I sign away my liberty? Never!"

Edward Phillips had not yet exhausted his fund of sarcasm: "Liberty! Liberty to drink rum! Liberty to reel through the streets! Liberty to roll in the gutter, to have a black eye and a bloated face, to have rags, poverty and contempt. Liberty to bruise one's wife and beggar one's children! To end up in the prison or on the gallows! Is this the liberty that our fathers bled and died for? Is this what our blessed Bible means when it says we are called unto liberty? Why, the pledge is the breaking of the prisoner's chains. It is the sign of liberty to be a sober, industrious, Christian man."

Charlie Brown was the next speaker: "Is it kind, is it polite, to ask others to sign a pledge that would be so hard for them to keep? Is it like a true wife to put down her name, and so place a bar between herself and her husband? Does not this interfere with the happiness of husband and wife?"

"Humph!" said Tommy Truman. "It would make my neighbor feel uncomfortable if I should paint my house, therefore I must let it remain as rusty as his. If a lady's husband swears, so must she; if he chews tobacco, so must she. It might interfere with their mutual happiness if she should pledge herself to Christ."

A bright-eyed little girl sat near Mr. Nelson. He suddenly turned toward her and said pleasantly, "Caroline, I have a request to make of you."

"A request?" she repeated, with wondering eyes.

"Yes. I want you to sign this pledge."

"Me? But I'm only seven; I am not in danger."

"Everyone is in danger, my child."

"Men and boys, you mean, Mr. Nelson."

"I mean women as well as men, girls as well as boys. You, young as you are, are not too young or too wise or too strong to escape. He 'goeth about as a roaring lion, seeking whom he may devour.' Besides, you have influence. Caroline, if you sign, you may save someone. If you refuse, you may ruin someone."

"If I really thought I had any influence or could be the means of helping anyone, I would sign it. I think I will do it, Mr. Nelson."

"Thank you," Mr. Nelson said. "More than this audience are rejoicing over your decision. Truman, will you pass the book this way?"

The young girl's cheeks flushed a deeper red, and

she said in some confusion: "Do you really mean I am to sign it now?"

"Why not? 'Do with thy might whatsoever thy hand findeth to do.'"

"But before all the people?"

"'Let your light so shine before men,'" quoted Mr. Nelson. And without more ado Caroline wrote her name.

"Now, Caroline, I wish I could get you and all young ladies to make one more promise: that you would never marry a man who refuses to sign the pledge."

This was evidently putting the matter a little too strongly for Tom Stuart: "But, Mr. Nelson," he said, "what if a man entirely worthy of Miss Caroline in every other respect, and truly loving her, refuses to sign the pledge? Should she have nothing to do with him?"

"I do not believe, Tom, that a man who will not shut and bolt the door between himself and strong drink ever does truly love, honor and respect a woman. That is talking strong ground, you think, but I have lived more years and watched this matter longer than you have. I tell you it is dangerous."

Caroline had been listening, her large eyes fixed intently on the speaker. Suddenly she said: "I promise. I do promise."

Mr. Nelson answered, "May God help you to keep your vows."

CHAPTER XIII

A STRANGE WITNESS

"I will never leave thee, nor forsake thee."

ell and Mr. Tresevant walked homeward, a fair share of the way in silence. Dell ventured a remark or two about the beauty of the evening, but she received absentminded replies and began to wonder why he did not go his own homeward way and commune with his own thoughts without disturbance, if such were his desire. At last she broke the silence and spoke in a mischievous tone: "Mr. Tresevant, why don't you criticize our performance this evening?"

"How do you know I am in a critical mood?" he asked quietly.

"Oh, I think you disapprove of a dozen things that were said and done. I can see it in your face; the moonlight is very bright, you know. Besides, I looked at you twice during the evening."

He laughed, then spoke gravely. "Since you read my face so well, I may as well confess to you that I did disapprove of the tenor of the arguments. I do not know whom I am censuring, probably Mr. Nelson. He is not a Christian man, though he speaks as one; we must not expect much of him. But I wish he were more careful of his choice of language."

"It was not his language at all," Dell said. "The exercise was selected."

"Well, in his selections then. I think it was a most unfortunate thing." Mr. Tresevant was growing excited, while Dell remained composed and goodhumored. She had not expected Mr. Tresevant to be pleased, knowing perfectly well that the arguments trenched too closely on his views.

"Please, enlighten me as to the unfortunateness of our evening's work," she said, still speaking gaily. "We are pluming ourselves on the fact that it passed off delightfully, and perhaps it is as well to have our pride somewhat subdued."

"I know you are not in sympathy with my views, Miss Bronson. I honor your deep convictions. You have good reason for them. But aside from your personal feeling, let me ask you, do you think it right to hold the pastor of a church up to ridicule before his own young people, be the subject what it may? May he not honestly differ in opinion with one member of his congregation without being made the subject of public sarcasm?"

Dell was surprised and dismayed. "Mr. Tresevant, I assure you nothing of the sort was intended or implied. I know the principal actors would be shocked and grieved if they supposed you imagined such a thing."

Mr. Tresevant smiled loftily. "I do not doubt your sincerity, but allow me to remind you that I am older than you and have probably seen more of the wrong side of the world. You are kind enough to believe that the exercise of the evening was selected. I believe nothing of the sort. I consider Mr. Nelson entirely capable of having written it, and I have not the least doubt but that he did so, and that it was most closely and unkindly aimed at me. I confess I once thought him more of a gentleman than to be guilty of so small a thing, but I must change my mind."

Dell's voice lost its touch of dismay and grew cold. "You have a right to believe what you please, a right you seem bent on gratifying, so I do not know that you will believe me when I tell you that Mr. Nelson never heard one word of the exercise until this evening. It was prepared by my Uncle Edward and me before I had so much as heard of your existence. So I am at a loss to understand how it could be considered a personal attack, unless it touched you so nearly that you must accept it as such."

It was Mr. Tresevant's turn to be dismayed. "Miss Bronson, I beg your pardon! I did not imagine — I assure you I had no idea — I do hope you will overlook my language." His face was red with shame.

"There is no occasion to apologize," Dell said, her good humor intact. "Actually, you have quite honored me in appropriating my wisdom to Mr. Nelson. Now, if I have proved to you that personality was the furthest from my thoughts, I have fairly earned the right to hear your criticisms."

"I am sorry that while I admire the talent displayed, I must be frank and not approve of some of the arguments," he answered.

"I am not sorry at all. I knew you would not

approve. What I want to know now is the reason why."

Hoping for a pleasant end to the evening, Mr. Tresevant wanted to lay the matter at rest. "Miss Bronson, haven't we been over this ground before?"

"Not a bit," Dell said. "The arguments are not old ones; I think we advanced a few that are original. Now for your objections."

He spoke reluctantly. "I do not approve of exacting indiscriminate promises, especially from the young, for any purpose whatever."

"Nor do I. But how does your remark apply to us? The promise asked for tonight after our exercise applied to something very definite, very simple, and it had been very carefully explained."

"Do you really think the promise extorted from that child tonight, in regard to her future marriage, is likely to be kept, provided it conflicts with her future wishes?"

"I don't know," Dell answered. "But, Mr. Tresevant, the same child united with your church two weeks ago. Do you expect she will keep the solemn promise that you — I will not say extorted from her, although I think there certainly was as much appearance of extortion as there was in our meeting this evening?"

"If she does keep it," he answered her in some heat and ignoring the question she asked, "if she does keep it, I think you have laid her under a cruel obligation — one that may be the cause of great and unnecessary suffering. The man who seeks her for a wife may be in every way worthy of her and yet have conscientious scruples against signing a pledge. How can you think it right to fetter people thus?"

Dell laughed, but she immediately apologized for

it. "I beg your pardon, Mr. Tresevant. You have a right to your own views, and I suppose I have a right to consider them absurd if I choose. But if you wish me to define my opinion, it is simply that a good man who has considered the evils of intemperance, who has resolved in his heart and asked God to help him put down the evil, is in my estimation solemnly pledged. If he is conscientiously opposed to putting his name on a piece of paper, he is a mystery to be sure. But a man who was conscientiously opposed to pledges because he believed in temperance as opposed to total abstinence, because he liked wine or beer or cider and meant to use it, I certainly would not marry. I would do anything in my power to keep a friend of mine from marrying him. Those are my solemn convictions, Mr. Tresevant."

He answered her lightly, without a trace of his former interest. "Miss Bronson, I propose that you and I raise a flag of truce. We shall probably never agree any better than we do now in our views on this subject, and we certainly can find pleasanter topics to discuss. I beg your pardon for having drawn you into this debate; I will endeavor not to do so again." Then followed a few bright words from each in regard to other matters, and he left her at her father's door.

She went to her little back parlor and dropped herself wearily into a seat. She grew suddenly tired. She had worked hard and eagerly for this evening. She had assumed much care and responsibility, and what had been accomplished? Nothing, it seemed to her. She even wondered if the exercise had been a failure; if only Uncle Edward had been there to help and comment.

"If only he were here now," this poor lonely girl

said aloud. "Or if I were there, sitting on the low seat by Aunt Laura and Uncle Edward, going over the evening and pointing out what we could do to improve the next effort. Uncle and Auntie, I need you. Oh, stop!" This last as a sort of rallying cry to her drooping heart. "You must not desert me," she said to her weary spirits. "This is not Boston, and I am not with my aunt and uncle. I am here alone, and I must do what I can and be cheerful about it," she resolved. And, gathering up her fallen hat and gloves, she walked out into the hall.

There was much loud talking in the barroom, and she could distinguish her father's voice and her own name. "My Dell will beat all the singing you ever heard tell of," he was saying. "I declare, if you shan't have a sample," and just as Dell was passing the door, he swung it open and spoke to her.

"I declare, here you are! I'm in the very nick of time. I was coming to hunt you. Just you come in now and give us a song. Steve here has been bragging like all possessed about his girl's singing, and I tell him I know she can't begin to compare with mine, and I want you to come and prove it." Saying which he took hold of her arm and tried to draw her in. Dell had to think very quickly. Her father had been drinking, not so much as he often did but enough to render him incapable of seeing the impropriety of his direction. There were four others in the barroom, all of them drunk. One of them, a young man, seemed to have some faint gleams of sense left, for he muttered: "Oh, now, Bronson, that's, that's rather mean taking advantage of a girl. Let her go now — that's a good fellow!"

What should she do? Here was her father, talking eagerly and gently pushing her in. Yet there was a wild gleam in his eye suggestive of anything but gentleness, and there was no means of determining what he might not do if his anger was aroused by refusal. Yet could she come into that awful room and sing for those four drunkards? Was there any hope that a song of hers might reach their hearts? Would she not in a sense be casting pearls before swine if she attempted to reach them while they were in their present condition? What would Uncle Edward tell her to do if he were there? Should she try to get away — and run the risk of maddening her father and losing the influence that she now had over him?

What would the Master tell her to do? "In season and out of season." Did it mean even at such times as these? Yes. Dell lifted up her heart in a brief, earnest cry for help, then allowed herself to be drawn into the room. Taking her station near the door and looking, in her white dress and white face, like a pale spirit descended among them from another world, she suddenly let her pure, rich voice float through the room. Her father dropped silently into a chair near her and listened as every word came to their ears distinctly:

> Say, sinner! hath a voice within
> Oft whispered to thy secret soul,
> Urged thee to leave the ways of sin,
> And yield thy heart to God's control?
>
> Sinner! it was a heavenly voice —
> It was the Spirit's gracious call;
> It bade thee make the better choice,
> And haste to seek in Christ thine all.

Spurn not the call to life and light;
Regard, in time, the warning kind;
That call thou mayst not always slight,
And yet the gate of mercy find.

Sinner, perhaps this very day,
Thy last accepted time may be;
Oh! shouldst thou grieve Him now away,
Then hope may never beam on thee.

Even Dell herself knew she had never sung so well before. Those words seemed to be wrung from her very soul, and her listeners sat as if they felt something of their power. Then silently and swiftly, as if she had indeed been a spirit, she turned and vanished from the room. She ran upstairs, through the hall to her own room and locked and bolted the door. She flung herself on her knees and buried her head in the pillow, giving way to a passion of tears as the bitterness of her lot rolled heavily upon her.

What a humiliation had come over her! What would her Boston friends have thought to have found her singing in a barroom to a company of drunkards? And one of them her father! She felt crushed and hopeless. What had she accomplished? What could she accomplish? Who was here in Lewiston to help her? Even the minister of the gospel turned away from the work — had no words for it but those of discouragement. Gradually the stormy grief subsided and her tears came quietly. After a little while there came to the lonely girl a sweet remembrance of the fact that she was not alone. There was really no such thing as lonely hours for her. Had not her Father said: "I will never leave thee, nor forsake thee"?

CHAPTER XIV

A TRIP
TO BOSTON

His ways are not as our ways.

t was another August day, hot and dusty and altogether uncomfortable for most people. Dell did not look uncomfortable. She stood framed in the doorway of the old depot, exactly where she stood the first time you ever heard of her. But for the fact that the linen suit was fresh and crisp, you might imagine we had gone backward in our story to Dell's entrée into Lewiston.

Yet she was really a year older and had not just alighted from the train but was standing there watching the man fasten the bit of brass to her neat little trunk that was to see it safe to Boston. It was a year to the day since she had stood there before and waited for her father. She thought of it, and it sent her mind wandering back over the year. How much she had meant to accomplish! A year had seemed to her a long time, and she had almost expected to work miracles. She both smiled and sighed as she thought of it that afternoon. Well, what had been accomplished? At times Dell's heart answered drearily, "Nothing, nothing." The old tavern still stood, and the dreadful bar still poured forth its poisons. Her father still drank his glasses of brandy, more glasses than he drank a year ago. From time to time Sam Miller still reeled home in the darkening twilight and whipped little Mamie and turned his wife out of doors. The loafers still spit and chewed in the barroom, just as many of them as before.

Mr. Tresevant still preached his Sunday sermons in the dreary church, still looked with grave, doubtful eyes on the temperance movement. Mr. Elliot still drank his wine, in a gentlemanly way when he was where respectable people could see him, and in a much more doubtful way sometimes, if report spoke truth. Yes, a looker-on would have said that all things remained as they were before.

No, not all things. The long, dirty piazza, where the spitting, chewing loafers had sat that day and stared at Dell, was now in a new coat of paint, spotlessly clean and absolutely bereft of loafers. There were things that Dell would not endure, and this, though apparently a trifle, was one of them. It was an innovation; the great leather-bottomed, high-backed armchairs had stood on that piazza as long and much longer than Dell could remember, and the chewing and spitting and chuckling had gone on from time immemorial. But when Dell had said, "They must do all such disgraceful work inside, Father; I cannot have it on my nice, clean piazza," her father had remembered certain other innovations, such as clean rooms and pleasant meals and no more fighting in the kitchen. He had chuckled a little, admiring his daughter immensely, and declared it should be as she said. So the piazza was purified, and the young men who boarded in the house came up clean steps, without the smell of tobacco or whiskey.

A little thing, to be sure, but there were other little things. Sally and Kate in the kitchen stood ready to fall down and worship their mistress; they did everything in their power to aid her efforts. Then the temperance meeting, weak and small though it was, still lived, and several had joined them that they did not expect — among others, the post office clerk who boarded at the hotel and used to take an occasional glass of wine. Then — and Dell's eyes brightened as she thought of it — her class, those five wild young men, was her class still. Reformed, you ask? Become patterns to the rising youth of America? Very little of that, but they came to Sunday school — came every Sunday — and were attentive and respectful to her, though hardly so to anyone else. Dell prayed for them all, now hopefully, now despairingly, always persistently.

Mr. Tresevant came briskly down the street, sprang up the depot steps and held out his hand to Dell. "You meant to be in time, did you not, Miss Dell? I called to walk with you to the cars, but you had already left. I wanted to see you off."

Dell laughed. "How kind of you. I was in haste. It seemed to me I should get on faster if I took an early start, but I don't see that I have made great speed thus far. Isn't the train late, Mr. Tresevant?"

"Not yet, certainly. It isn't due for ten minutes. What haste you are in to leave Lewiston! Has it then no attraction whatever for you? Are you always going to feel there is no place in the world but Boston?" He spoke half reproachfully, half — was it regret?

Dell had no answer for him, as her eyes drew her attention to the young man approaching the cellar rum shop across the street. She watched him until he neared the door, and then the only reply Mr. Tresevant received was an eager "Isn't that Jim Forbes, Mr. Tresevant? Yes, I know it is." She called in clear, quick tones, "Mr. Forbes."

If a bombshell had exploded just ahead of him, the young man could not have turned more suddenly than he did at the sound of that voice. He came across the street, and Dell came down from the doorway and stood on the second step, smiling and cordial.

"Did you come up to see me off?" she asked, holding out her hand, which he grasped as if his had been an iron vise.

"No," he said with an awkward laugh. "Not exactly. I come to see myself off. I've got to go down to Boston to get an iron fixed."

"And you are going on this train? Why, then, I shall not have to travel alone after all."

Meantime Mr. Tresevant, after an impatient frown or two, had risen above himself and come forward to greet Jim Forbes. He did not offer to shake hands with him. Truth to tell, he did not know the rough young fellow well enough to venture, but his greeting was sufficiently kind, and Jim received it with an awkward attempt at courtesy.

"Mr. Forbes is going to Boston on this train," explained Dell. "So I shall have someone to escort me."

Then there came over Mr. Tresevant a suffocating sense of the fact that he, being a minister of the gospel, ought to say something improving to this young man. But he said the last thing Dell would have had him say if she could have chosen. "You must keep away from all such places as that which I saw you about to enter if you are going to take care of the ladies, my boy."

The "boy" blushed to the roots of his very red hair but answered promptly enough. "That's easier said than done, when there's one of them places at every corner and folks hanging around to coax a fellow in."

"That is true," Dell said. "But, Mr. Forbes, there is coaxing on the other side too, remember. Don't you know how much I want you to join our temperance society? It would be a help to you as well as to us." Saying which, she looked wistfully at Mr. Tresevant, hoping he would in this one case see the merit of a pledge and join his persuasion to hers. But Mr. Tresevant looked down at his boots and was silent.

As for Jim Forbes, he only blushed the harder and muttered, "I dunno about that." And then the train shrieked in, and in a very few minutes out again, taking Dell and her escort with it.

Dell settled herself into a seat and made room for Jim beside her. He, however, preferred the arm of the seat and stationed himself thereon. Gradually Dell became unpleasantly conscious that she was attracting attention. Here was a neat, trim, becomingly dressed maiden. Beside her sat a tall, ungainly, tanned youth in a soiled factory shirt, minus collar and cravat, and with a well-worn coat hanging on his arm. As he talked earnestly to her, the stares became frequent, and an occasional comment was loud.

At a stop near Boston, the Chesters — the three young ladies and Mr. Will Chester — boarded, greeting Dell eagerly.

"Why, Dell! Dell Bronson! What a delight to see you again. Are you coming home to stay? Only a week! How awful. Oh, Dell, we can't let you go away again." And then they turned wondering eyes on poor Jim.

Will Chester leaned forward and whispered: "Isn't that fellow offensive to you? Shall I suggest his removal?"

Dell, flushing almost as deeply as Jim himself, answered quickly, "Oh, no. I know him very well." She turned again to Jim with a cordial "Finish telling me about that evening now, will you?" And the Chesters stared and wondered and whispered.

At the next station there came the De Quincys. Now the De Quincys had been in the habit of, well, not exactly turning their aristocratic heads away from Dell (Mr. Edward Stockwell's niece was not a lady to be turned away from, even by the De Quincys); but they thought her "exceedingly peculiar" and were rarely in sympathy with her "singular" movements. They came over to greet her and to assure her that Boston had missed her. And then Jim endured some fearful staring, and Miss Helen De Quincy whispered, "Is that dreadful creature intoxicated? Why don't you appeal to the conductor?"

"Because," said Dell, all her blushing embarrassment gone and her eyes brimming with mischief, "because I have no need of his services. The gentleman is a particular friend of mine." To tell the truth, Dell heartily enjoyed shocking the De Quincys.

At last the train steamed into the Boston depot. Two minutes more and the tall form of Mr. Edward

Stockwell was gently forcing its way through the crowd. Even the De Quincys stepped a little to one side to let him pass. There were very few who were not willing to yield to Mr. Edward Stockwell.

"Oh, Uncle!" Dell said breathlessly, with very bright, yet very moist eyes.

And the voice, gentle and tender yet with a sense of strength about it, answered: "Darling child."

And Dell knew she was at home once more. She turned suddenly to her companion and said, "Uncle Edward, this is Mr. Forbes."

Mr. Stockwell's keen eye lighted with a genial smile. "One of your class," he said instantly. "I remember the name. Welcome to Boston, Mr. Forbes. Thank you for taking care of my niece." And Jim Forbes felt his hand held in such a cordial, kindly grasp as he had never known in all his life before. Both the De Quincys and the Chesters stared.

"Now," said Uncle Edward as the train stopped at last, "we can go, I think. One, two, three. Any more, Dell? Mr. Forbes, if you will take the traveling bag, I will manage the rest." And so Mr. Forbes made his first awkward essay in waiting on a lady.

"Where do you stop?" asked Mr. Stockwell as they neared his carriage. "Any place in view? Oh, let me direct you then, will you? I'll find you a very convenient place; just take a seat in the carriage. I'm going directly past where you would like to be. Oh, certainly get in; there's plenty of room. It's no trouble at all. A friend of Miss Bronson's is a friend of mine."

And Jim Forbes leaned back among the puffy cushions, wondering as they whirled through the streets what would happen to him next and what Joe and Tom and the others would think if they could see him now.

At a certain point Mr. Stockwell stopped the carriage and sprang out. Entering a building where a dozen men were writing in the front room, he said, "Mr. Lewis, I want to see Carey a moment." From an inner office a brisk young man was promptly summoned.

"Carey," said Mr. Stockwell, "Miss Dell has come, and in company with her is a young man from the country. Can you get him in at your boarding place and help him through with his business? He is a very rough young fellow. Needs especially to avoid saloons and the like."

"I'll look after him, sir," the young man said. "Where shall I find him?"

"Here, in my carriage." Mr. Stockwell meantime drew his pocketbook and placed a bill in the young man's hand. "And, Carey, have you some pleasant place of entertainment and employment for the evening?"

"Yes, sir, but I have funds on hand."

"Never mind — this will do for another time then. Come to the carriage at once, please. Mr. Lewis, you will excuse Carey for the remainder of the day, if you please.

"Mr. Forbes," Uncle Edward continued, being now at the carriage door, "I have a friend here who will look after your comfort with pleasure. Mr. Carey, Mr. Forbes. You return tomorrow, I think you said? Will you call at my office in the morning? Mr. Carey will show you the way. Good afternoon, and thank you again for your kindness."

"Uncle Edward?" Dell said, clasping her hands in delight as the carriage door shut them in together. "That is just splendid. How did you remember all about this boy and know what ought to be done for him?"

"It is part of my business, dear child, in the employ of my Master, to remember people's names and study their character, as far as possible."

"Uncle Edward, it isn't possible to help my boys in Lewiston; it is just a little bit of a village. But if they were all here in Boston, I could help to save them. There are such programs and rallies and energy here, although I suppose there is a great deal of wickedness too. But in Lewiston there is not a living soul to help them. No one who has any interest in them."

"What has become of Mr. Nelson?"

"He would if he could," Dell said thoughtfully. "But, Uncle, there are no resources to do it with."

"Then it is the facilities that you lack, not the living soul. In regard to that, dear child, isn't God in Lewiston? Have you forgotten that He has facilities to work with that we know not of?"

CHAPTER XV

THE REVIEW

"Teach me thy way, O Lord."

inner again in the dainty Boston dining room, so fair and pure in all its details, rested and soothed Dell's beauty-starved heart. After dinner they went into the back parlor, where they used to linger together on summer evenings. And Dell, mindful of how many times she had longed for that seat, went straight to the low ottoman, wheeled it in front of Aunt Laura's chair and snugged herself into it. Aunt Laura's left hand fondly smoothed the soft bands of brown hair, just as Dell had known it would, just as she had imagined the touch endless times during the long days of that past year.

Uncle Edward had brought pen and paper and occupied a table at the west window. When his wife frowned on the business implements, he said: "Just a very little writing, my dear. I have brought it here so I can imagine myself visiting with you. We must make the most of Dell. It is only a week, you know. I shall be through very soon, and meantime you may talk or play as the mood takes you. It will not disturb me in the least."

So they talked — one of their long talks in the quiet twilight. By and by the twilight deepened. Aunt Laura asked Dell to play the piano for them — Dell's dear piano, for which her fingers had fairly ached during the year of separation. She touched the keys with a tremulous eagerness, and soft, plaintive sounds filled the room — sounds that made the writer over by the table pause and raise his head to listen. Presently he hurried the last line to its close, shut his ink stand with a click and, rising, moved a chair toward the piano.

"Now, dear child, the music is glorious, but tongues are aching to be used. Begin at the beginning and tell us about the year."

Dell wheeled around on the piano stool. Leaning forward, she rested her hand on his arm. "Oh, Uncle! The beginning? What a long story it will be! And yet very short. It has been a long year, and I have tried to do a great many things, and I have done none of them. That, after all, is the whole story in a nutshell."

"But I don't want it in a nutshell. I want the whole story spread out, detailed. Unless you have greatly changed, you know how to do it. Has Lewiston changed much? I haven't seen it in eight years, you know."

"Uncle, it has changed backward. It is the meanest, dullest place I have ever seen. There is no paint on the buildings and no posts to the fences. They have rotted and tumbled over. And the church — I can't even describe that to you! Why, your carriage house would make a delightful house compared with it. And there is a rum hole at every corner — some between corners. I never saw such a place."

"Yet the people are not poor?"

"Poor? No, indeed! There is wealth enough in the place to revolutionize it. But the people have no enthusiasm for anything but their stores and factories and saloons. Uncle Edward, what do you suppose God thinks of such Christians as there are in Lewiston?"

Uncle Edward looked up suddenly, smiled a kind, grave smile, laid a tender hand over the little one resting on his arm and said: "He has told you and me what to think about them. We must remember, 'Judge not, that ye be not judged; and with what measure ye mete, it shall be measured to you again!' What of your father, Dell?"

"There is nothing to say. Father is selling rum as usual and — drinking it," the last two words with lowered voice and burning cheeks.

"And what is our Dell doing for him just now?"

"There is nothing for me to do," she answered him sadly. "At least if there is I cannot find it. I have tried everything I can think of and failed in all."

"Then you are not praying for him anymore?"

"Oh, Uncle Edward!" she cried with a quick, startled look. "You know I did not mean that. I am praying for him constantly with all my heart, but that is all."

"Well, about the class. Are you encouraged?"

"Why, they come regularly, and they seem to like me. But as to any change in them, I see none. No, I can't say that I am encouraged. I am very heavy-hearted. What good for them to spend an hour a week in Sunday school if it doesn't influence their lives a particle?"

Uncle Edward waived the question. "Is Mr. Tresevant any help to you?"

Dell's eyes flashed. "No, sir, he isn't; he is a drawback in this case. I have written you about Mr. Elliot, haven't I? Well, I believe he could be persuaded to join our society but for Mr. Tresevant's influence; he actually uses it against us. Mr. Tresevant is certainly likeable enough, always pleasant, and we converse happily on other topics. But we cannot speak of this one issue, which is the passion of my life. Uncle, do you see how a good man in these days can stand silent, even work against the temperance cause?"

"No, my dear, I don't. I believe him to be mistaken; I pray the Lord will someday set him right. One more question: What of Mr. Nelson?"

"He is the same mystery he was at first — working faithfully, and apparently conscientiously, yet without conscientious motives. Indeed, Uncle, we are all just what we were a year ago."

"Is that possible?" her uncle asked with an earnest, searching look. "My dear daughter, I have asked many questions about others; now, concerning you. Have you, darling, gone onward in a year's time? Do you find your faith stronger, your trust firmer, your heart and life more entirely hid with Christ in God?"

Dell's head went suddenly down on the arm against which she leaned. Her bright eyes filled with tears. He waited quietly, and presently she raised her head again. "Uncle Edward, I don't know. Sometimes it seems to me I have gone backward. I have tried to work for Christ. I know I have that end in view, but it seems to me almost a wasted year. And there are times when I want to run away from it all and hide with you and Aunt Laura. There are times when I am utterly impatient and rebellious and think I have done all I can; it is time there was some fruit. So a great deal of the time I am not happy, and yet I don't quite know what is wrong."

He answered the young girl's wistful look with a kind smile. "Do you want me to pick your work to pieces, dear child, as I used to when you were indeed a child?"

"Indeed, Uncle Edward, I want your help. I have wanted it more than I can tell you."

"Then, my dear, I shall have to tell you that I think the main trouble with you has been a too vivid realization of the person called 'I.' I do not mean you are troubled with egotism. I do not consider that one of your faults. Nor do I mean that you have too strong a sense of personal responsibility — but that your temptation is to forget you are a worker with God. It is a temptation common to us all: you grow discouraged; you think your efforts have been failures.

"Here — two or three questions you might ask yourself carefully: First, am I really engaged in a work in which I believe the Lord Himself is interested? If so, is He discouraged, or has His working with me been a failure? That puts the failure in a very startling form, you see. Our own shortcomings we have reason to lament, not by sitting with folded arms, wasting precious time while we mourn, but with the true sorrow that says, 'God helping me, I will not make that mistake again or leave that duty undone tomorrow.' To lament over the non-accomplishment of a work, our part of which we have honestly and earnestly tried to do, is to forget the fact that when our part is done, it is God who does the rest.

"You may depend upon it, dear child, that the Lord wants that dear father of yours and Mr. Nelson and all your class to be numbered among His jewels quite as much as you. He has ways and means with which to bring about His ends that you and I dream not of. You must drop that overtasked, much-encumbered 'I' out of your thoughts and learn to say 'We.' Think much about the partnership. Speak it over often to yourself, reverently indeed, but yet triumphantly: 'God and I.' "

"But ought I not to feel a deep interest in, even anxiety about, these souls in danger?"

"Being a young, impetuous Christian, you will doubtless have much of this feeling to struggle with. But there is a more blessed resting place. Resting in the Lord. You know the direction 'and having done all, to stand'? And another, 'Wait on the Lord: be of good courage, and he shall strengthen thine heart: wait, I say, on the Lord'? We have many directions about that sort of waiting, and your eager heart needs to learn the lesson carefully."

A little silence fell between them. Dell's hand sought Aunt Laura's and was clasped firmly. Finally she looked up with bright eyes and said, "Thank you, Uncle Edward. You have given me the help I needed."

"If you follow my advice, I think you will find yourself rested. There is no more solemn or needed prayer for us than that which our elder Brother left among His latest, 'Not as I will, but as thou wilt.' "

Then a sudden change of subject. "Have you really decided, Dell, that you cannot accompany us

to the seaside for a short holiday? We have counted
on it."

Dell answered him with her old, bright smile:
" 'And having done all, to stand.' There is work for
me to do, Uncle."

He laid his hand on her head and answered,
" 'The Lord, before whom I walk, will send His angel
with thee and prosper thy way.' "

The days that followed were like flashes of sunlight — the beauty and joy and rest of which Dell
never forgot. They were so unlike the dull, shivery,
rainy one on which she rubbed the train-car window
with her handkerchief, trying to catch one glimpse
of the retreating form of her Uncle Edward. As he
drew his cloak about him and bent his umbrella
forward to shield himself from the downpour, she
half wondered if the time that had seemed such a
tiny week to her had not after all been months,
whirling her right into the middle of November
dreariness. But it wasn't; it was only one of those
August foretastes of what November can do. Dell
struggled with her homesick heart. She tried not to
think of the differences between Lewiston and Boston as the train shrieked in alongside the Lewiston
depot.

She clambered out alone, bargained for a seat in
the mail wagon and thanked a stranger for sharing
his umbrella.

When she landed in the hall at home, which despite all her rearrangements looked dingy enough,
she resolutely put from her the thought of that other
long, wide, beautiful hall. To her father's greeting,
"Well, and so you are here!" she answered cheerily,
"Yes, I'm here." She went straight over to him and
bestowed a hearty kiss on the rough, red face, then

went up to her own room. Again she needed to shut out comparisons and cheer herself with something. Out loud and firmly she told herself, "Wait on the Lord: be of good courage, and he shall strengthen thine heart: wait, I say, on the Lord."

Some fruit from that Boston visit had already ripened, if Dell had but known it. Jim Forbes, walking down to the factory with his friend and companion Cooley, gave a detailed account of his Boston experience and finished it on this wise: "Him and her both couldn't have treated me no better if I'd been a prince, and I'll tell you what my mind is made up to, Cooley. I'm going to sign that there pledge the very next meeting they have — blamed if I don't." And he did.

CHAPTER XVI

The Proposal

"But he knoweth the way that I take."

everal months had passed in our girl's life since she returned from that heartening week in Boston. Her influence had by now been felt by more members of Lewiston society. The temperance cause had grown in numbers, if not in strength.

Sally and Kate were still as much a part of Dell's scheme to persuade her father in the right direction; they had, in fact, attended recent meetings, and Sally hinted that she might sign her name to the pledge, if she felt so inclined.

Jonas Bronson found more and more to be pleased with in his daughter. A glance here and there took in all that he wanted to see; the slightest word spoken on rare occasions encouraged Dell's heart even the least bit.

Mr. Nelson was still wavering in the balances regarding spiritual concerns, and Mr. Tresevant had come no closer to signing the pledge. But in those foregoing months the young minister had grown closer to Dell, and she to him.

Lewiston was simmering in the heat of summer when Dell received a welcome call from the minister, though an edge of tension soon cut through the air.

Mr. Tresevant stood over by the mantel. His face was very pale, and his lips were pressed tightly together, as if he were trying to control some strong emotion. Dell sat in a low chair at a little distance, plucking the petals of a great pink rose. The pink on her cheek was deepened to a vivid crimson, and the hands that pulled apart the heart of the rose trembled visibly.

When Mr. Tresevant finally spoke, his voice was low and constrained. "It is a most singular idea of duty — one that I cannot comprehend. I trust too entirely in your truth to believe for a moment that it is a mere excuse, that you are hiding your real feelings from me. But is it not a trivial question to come between us?"

"Not trivial to me, Mr. Tresevant. I thought you understood my position on this question. I surely have reason to consider it in a solemn light."

"Miss Bronson, I do not interfere with your views on the question. I have even told you that I respect them. What more would you have?"

"But you are not in sympathy with them?"

"I do not carry my ideas to the same length as you, that is all. Surely, as a sensible woman, you do not require this of any man. I do not ask it of you."

"I ask it," she said with trembling lips. "On this one subject I ask it. I dare not do without it."

There was a touch of bitterness in his tone. "Dell, do you really consider me in danger of becoming a drunkard because I do not deem it proper to sign a total abstinence pledge?"

His tone seemed to give her strength. She gave him the benefit of a full look into the depths of her great earnest eyes as she answered: "I do not consider it impossible. I have known men as secure as you seem to be who have fallen victims. I do not consider any man safe who is not an absolute foe to liquor in all its forms. But it is not even that which presents itself most forcibly to me. We are truly not in sympathy in regard to this thing. I have felt it keenly during the progress of our acquaintance. How much more sharply do you think I would feel it if my life were part of yours?

"There is another thing," she continued. "I cannot feel that your views on this subject are right. I cannot feel that God will bless you in them. By your silence and example you stand in the way of men who you know are in danger, even if you are not, and you do not put forth a helping finger. You even encourage them in their evil way. You do this very thing with Mr. Elliot. You must know that he is in danger, and you know what an influence you have over him; yet how do you use it? Even now I look on with grief. I feel powerless to help it. Sometimes it almost drives me wild. How do you think I could endure it under other circumstances?"

"You exaggerate difficulties," he said, struggling with his own heart and trying to speak calmly. "It is your nature to do so. You are excitable and easily moved to extremes. You're seeing mountains where only molehills exist. Young Elliot, for instance, is safe enough. He's a little fast for a young man in his position, but I'm doing what I can to restrain him, and I hope to succeed in the end.

"Indeed I don't think I deserve to be judged as harshly as you are judging me. I am trying in my way to do good in the world, even if it is not quite like your way. May the Master not own it after all?"

Dell lowered her eyes to the torn rose in her lap then lifted her face to meet his. Her voice was very humble in answer. "I do not want you or anyone to work 'in my way.' I have asked God to show me His way. It is not a method of work but a principle that we are speaking of. I consider total abstinence from everything that intoxicates a solemn Christian duty. You do not think any such thing. Now, Mr. Tresevant, how could we possibly agree?"

"By agreeing to disagree. You have a full and perfect right to think as you do, and, thinking so, you are right in working to your views of duty. I accord this right to you. Can't you do the same by me?"

"But can we both be right and moving in opposite directions? Is there no such thing as an enlightened conscience guiding toward the only right way? If I choose to think that breaking the Sabbath is a proper thing to do, have I a full and perfect right to do so? And would you accord me that right?"

"The cases are not parallel in the least," he said, changing his position uneasily. "The one is a plain scriptural injunction that we have no right to question. The other is only a difference of opinion."

"Now you have reached the very point where we should differ the most. I consider the one scriptural injunction as plain and unquestionable as the other. When I hear my own poor father quoting the fact that you drink cider as an excuse for his business and habits, can you wonder that I think the solemn declaration 'If meat make my brother to offend, I will eat no flesh while the world standeth' as binding upon Christians as that other command, 'Remember the Sabbath day, to keep it holy'? The first is not, it is true, in the form of a command. But should a Christian follow only commands without regard to the spirit of the gospel?"

"That is true," he said gently. "But, Dell, the precise path in which a man should walk is not always marked out for him in the Bible. He is left to be guided by his conscience, and you must learn to think that those who differ from your peculiar views may be conscientious in doing so. Perhaps," he added, with a halfhearted attempt at a smile, "it may be part of your mission to reform me. I will try to be a faithful pupil. Won't you take me in hand?"

But Dell could not control her voice to answer him. A sudden mist swam before her eyes. She looked down at the rose petals in utter silence. Her companion turned suddenly from his position by the mantel, pushed an ottoman just in front of her and sat down.

"Dell," he said softly. "Dear friend, won't you think this through again and see if you can afford, for a mere trifling difference of opinion, to destroy your life and mine? You have told me you love me, and surely I have offered you no mean gift — the strong, true, abiding love of a manly heart. I feel that I need you. I need your help and sympathy in my work. I believe God would bless us in our efforts to work unitedly for Him. It can't be possible that you will let a very trifle come between us. Can you afford to be so indifferent to God's crowning gift — human love?"

The deep crimson glow went out entirely from

Dell's cheek, leaving it marble-like in its whiteness. A vivid sense of the solitude of her life rushed over her. A vivid sense of the love and care and protection this strong human arm offered for her to lean upon surged in upon her. Why not let herself be so blessed? Why should she be shut out from this crowning gift of God? She trembled with the great longing to follow the pleading of her own heart. Why not? He was a good man, a Christian man — she did not doubt that in the least. Why let this trifle separate them? It was a trifle surely.

From the not-distant barroom came voices many and loud, some oaths mingling with the coarse words and raucous laughter. Her father's voice, distinctly marked above the others, came full upon her ear, loud and thick. She shivered with pain; if all that could be banished from the world, what a father he might be! Yet here was this man sitting before her, his pale, pure face looking anxiously into hers. This man, asking for her hand in marriage, thought the temperance movement a misguided sort of fanaticism; thought that Christian men might be educated to a moderate use of liquors. Should she, whose life was pledged for a hand-to-hand struggle with what she believed to be the monster evil of the world, link that life with such lukewarmness as this?

She drew a long, heavy sigh. Bending slightly forward, she spoke with suppressed emotion: "Mr. Tresevant, I feel to my very soul the honor you have done me. I have given you proof of that, in that I have confessed to you that my heart answers, as my conscience will not. My life is pledged to a certain work in which you do not believe. If I became your wife, I feel I could not do the work which I have promised God that I would try to do."

"It is incomprehensible to me," he said in a low, placid tone after a few moments of utter silence. "It is incomprehensible to me, if you feel toward me what you profess, that you can let this strange chimera come between us."

She searched his face, then said quietly: "Is it any stranger than that you, professing to think almost as I do, should not be willing to yield one inch of your views to help me in what is such a solemn, terrible thing to me?"

Mr. Tresevant pushed his seat back with a sudden jerk. He was not a meek man by nature, and he had been greatly humiliated. For the past two hours he had been keeping himself under control.

He spoke quickly and bitterly: "I will not be forced into signing a pledge for any woman on earth, not even you."

A perfect shower of rose petals torn in tiny bits fell at his feet. Dell stood and with steady eyes looked into his. She was not meek by nature either. And she had the advantage of him in that she knew he could not argue even to his own satisfaction in favor of his position. Her voice was clear and firm. "Then, Mr. Tresevant, we seem to understand each other. I can only repeat what I have told you before. I can never marry a man who will not set himself on the side of God and humanity in fighting against this awful wickedness."

Mr. Tresevant rose without another word, walked over to a side table and possessed himself of his hat. He came back to Dell and spoke in low, husky tones. "Good-bye," he said, to which he received no answer and seemed to expect none, for he turned away and went out the open door and down the street.

As for Dell, you may think she leaned her head on

the window seat and shed bitter tears. She didn't; such was not her nature. She looked at the fastenings of the blinds, drew down the shades and turned on the flame of the lamp a little more, noticing for the first time that it smoked. Then she went to the kitchen and gave her directions to Sally about the morning meal as calmly as if she did not realize she had just put from her the dearest and best thing that earthly life could ever offer her. On her way back she stopped to see that her father's room was in order.

At her own room, she locked herself in, turned down the light and sat down to look the events of the evening squarely in the face. None the less for her outward composure did she carry a very heavy heart. The long, blank future stretched out dully before her; she had turned away from the joy and blessedness held out for her. She realized with clarity what she might have been.

She was not sorry for her evening's work, not in the least. She had nerved herself for the task. Her words had not been spoken under the impulse of the moment. They had been carefully and prayerfully rehearsed when she saw that this question was to come to her. There might have been a little lingering hope that Mr. Tresevant's prejudices were not so deeply rooted as they had seemed — that he was more in sympathy with her work than she had thought — but never an instant's hesitancy as to her duty in the matter, except during that one breathless moment down in the parlor.

That was all past. She had asked God to show her the right way, and she believed He had — so there was nothing to regret. But she could not help thinking that threescore and ten was a very long time for people to live. She even wondered sadly what those people did who had to live seven, eight and nine hundred years in the olden times. She was thankful that no such lot would be hers. There was a great deal of work to do, and she must not shirk it. But when it was all done, or, better still, if the time should come soon for her to leave it all — come through no seeking of hers but because the King wanted His daughter at court and called her home — how pleasant it would be. She had no tears to shed; her heart felt too heavy for tears. But she took her one unfailing friend, her little well-worn Bible, and turned its leaves rapidly — no loitering tonight over precious verses here and there. She knew what she needed and turned straight to it.

"God is our refuge and strength, a very present help in trouble." She felt herself in trouble. She had asked to be led, and she felt that God was leading her. She did not murmur, but the way He had chosen for her feet seemed very hard.

CHAPTER XVII

LITTLE
MAMIE

*"How unsearchable are his judgments,
and his ways past finding out!"*

ll day long Dell Bronson had been in and out of Sam Miller's house — moving with that quick yet soft tread which betokens there is much to do and need for the quietness that prevails when a solemn stranger is being entertained. She had spent much time there during the last three days. She came in now bearing a host of white flowers and took them to the inner room. Mrs. Miller followed her, and the two stood together looking down on little Mamie.

The child had never lain in so beautiful a resting place before, and surely no sleep could be sounder or sweeter than that which held the eyelids closed and wreathed a faint smile around the quiet mouth. Little Mamie had suffered her last stroke for the cause of rum. She would never shiver and pale again because of her father's unsteady step. In her delicate coffin she slept undisturbed. Dell showered the flowers over her, placed a tiny white bud in her little waxen hand, then stood waiting in silence while the mother studied through tears the features of her lost darling.

"She is too sweet to be put in the ground," she moaned. "Only see what a smile is on her face, and she holds the flower as though she had been looking at it when she dropped asleep. Oh, I can't have her buried in the ground! Oh, Miss Bronson, she is too sweet and pretty for that."

"She is not too sweet for heaven," Dell said tenderly. "You must not think of her as buried in the ground; you cannot imagine how beautiful the place is that she has gone to." But Mrs. Miller's heart was too sore for comfort.

"I wanted her to live," she sobbed. "I needed her. I knew she could do what I couldn't. She was fond of her father, Miss Bronson. You can't think how she loved him, and he loved her too; folks needn't think he didn't, for he did. He was like a lamb with her always, when he was himself, and she could coax him to do 'most anything she wanted him to. She had begun to coax him to go to them temperance meetings of yours, and, Miss Bronson, you know he went once. I know she could have got him over on the right side if she could only have lived, but now he'll go to ruin faster than ever. God knows I wish I was dead and laid in the coffin with my darling."

And then the great scalding tears burst forth afresh and dropped on the waxen face before her. So natural the little one looked that it seemed she would put up her hand to wipe away the tears. What was there for Dell to say? The way looked dark enough, certainly. The mother's one comfort in life had been her fair-haired, sweet-faced Mamie. And Dell knew how, aside from all the love that the mother heart lavished on her one lamb, there was always the hope that the father would be won over from his evil ways by this child. He loved her. Dell, who had seen them often together, did not in the least doubt it. And now nothing seemed more probable than that — stung by terrible remorse, goaded by every blow that he ever let fall on the frail child, especially by those last blows only the night before Mamie was taken sick — he would plunge recklessly into drink to drown his misery. It was a dark way. She could not wonder that the poor mother wept and moaned over this open coffin, refusing to be comforted. There was but one ray of comfort; she returned again and again to that.

"But, Mrs. Miller, think — you have not lost her. She has only gone a little way, and isn't it good to remember that she will never suffer anymore? You know she had a great deal to suffer here, and that is all over now. No more pain or trouble of any kind for little Mamie."

Mrs. Miller rose up from her crouching posture beside the coffin and dried her eyes while she spoke rapidly, almost fiercely:

"You don't understand, Miss Bronson. You didn't know my Mamie as I knew her. She would have borne everything she did, yes, and a great deal more to save her father; that was her one thought, day and night. I don't understand it at all. I try to; I tried to take in what you've said to me about God hearing our prayers, and I've tried to pray. The other night I prayed all night long to Him to save my Mamie's life for her poor father's sake, and it all did no good.

Here she lies, dead. And her father will go to ruin. I suppose it must be so; but I can't understand it. I can't believe that she will be happy up there in heaven when she looks down and sees her father and mother miserable. She loved us so, you know."

Poor mourning mother! She had built her hopes on this fair bit of clay that lay motionless before her, and now she had nothing on which to cling. Dell stood looking at her with sad eyes, uncertain what to say or whether it would be well to say anything. At last she ventured timidly: "Mrs. Miller, there is one verse in the Bible that comforts me more than almost any other: His ways are not as our ways, it says, and I think of that constantly. When I make plans and God seems to come in between them and brush them all away, then I remember that He can certainly plan better than I. He wants the people of Lewiston. Wants them for His own, you know, a great deal more than I possibly can, and that quiets me."

Mrs. Miller only dimly understood her meaning. She knew nothing of the abiding trust that lived in Dell's heart, but she knew that Dell's father was in the same awful snare as her husband, and she knew that Dell's heart was heavy over it. She had come to understand the young girl during these months. They were waging war against a common foe, and while Dell worked for her father, Mrs. Miller knew that she still had given time and thought to Mamie's father. Thus it was that she had let this woman dress little Mamie for the last time and lay her in her coffin bed and cover her with flowers.

Everything was done now. The people were beginning to gather to the funeral, so Dell drew the poor mother away. What a pitiful thing it was, yet what a wonderful thing, this human love! Here was this mother looking her last on her one treasure, her only child, yet mourning chiefly even then for her husband, who had as surely been the means of placing her early in the narrow bed; it was as though one of his cruel blows had sent her suddenly to join the dead.

Thanks to Dell the house had been neatly and even tastefully arranged. Dell had tried to give it as little as possible the appearance of a drunkard's home. The burden was heavy enough to bear without exposing the wounds more than was necessary to the outside world.

The people were few and scattering who came to little Mamie Miller's funeral. The mother had said only a little while before, "Couldn't they sing a hymn, do you think? Mamie loved to hear singing so much." And Dell had answered, "Yes, they will sing a hymn."

So now she looked about her, somewhat startled to find that no choir appeared, as was the usual custom in Lewiston. Neither was there the choir director, Miss Emmeline Elliot. It had not occurred to her that they were not likely to come — because it was only Sam Miller's child. So when, after much looking about her and much questioning of Tommy Truman, she began to understand the matter, she turned with flashing eyes to Mr. Tresevant. She had not seen him, save in the pulpit, since that evening when he bade her good-bye, three weeks before. But she spoke to him now as though she had seen him but yesterday. "Mr. Tresevant, Mrs. Miller wishes to have singing."

"I don't know how to manage it," he said, looking troubled. "If I had known it before, I would have tried to induce some of the choir to come, but there is not one of them here."

"I can manage it," Dell said. "I will sing."

"Will you wish to sing entirely alone?" he asked her.

"No," she said, looking past him toward the doorway, where someone was entering. "Mr. Forbes will sing with me."

Now it chanced that Jim Forbes, mindful of his old friendship for Sam Miller and of sundry red-cheeked apples that he had given little Mamie, had asked and obtained an hour's leave of absence to attend the funeral. And it also chanced that Dell, sitting beside him in Sunday school, had occasionally heard him burst forth into splendid song, so now she went forward at once to claim his assistance. He was startled and confused and gratified all in one.

"But, Miss Bronson, I can't sing anything that you can," he said, blushing fiercely.

"Then I will sing something that you can," she answered quickly. "You can sing 'There is sweet rest in heaven,' for I've heard you. Well, we will sing that."

"But," said Mr. Tresevant, on being informed of the selection, "do you think that will be quite appropriate for so young a child?"

"Yes," said Dell, "entirely so. If anyone ever needed rest from the heavy burdens of life, it was poor little Mamie."

So it came to pass that never was a sweeter and more tender requiem more sweetly sung than that which floated around Mamie Miller's coffin. But Dell tried in vain to soften the despairing feelings in her heart and find appropriateness in the services that followed. "The Lord gave, and the Lord hath taken away; blessed be the name of the Lord!" quoted the clergyman; and Dell thought of the bruises and scars all over the poor little body and felt rebelliously that *rum* had taken her away. When he talked of the providence of God, she thought drearily of the bottle of rum in Sam Miller's closet. In vain she tried to make the service seem other than sacrilege; her faith was strong enough to grasp the thought that dear little Mamie was at rest, but it seemed to her overwrought heart that it was the earthly father's cruelty — not the heavenly Father's love — that had taken her from earth.

Very dark looked the world. Sam Miller's half-averted face and bloodshot eyes and the bowed mother's look of despair were alike suggestive of hopelessness. The clergyman's smooth, gentle tones, as he dwelt upon the great army of little children redeemed unto God, jarred painfully; the little children were safe and glad. Yes, she believed that, but the fathers, such as these, who had abused their trust and made it impossible for their little ones to stay with them — should they be soothed to rest and sleep by the words of peace? Dell had sunk to the depths where so many Christians often fall. She had lost sight of the truth that in spite of the woe and weariness of this wicked world, God reigns.

The small procession followed Mamie to the little grave under a maple tree. The father bit his white lips until they bled, and the mother moaned as they lowered the tiny coffin. The minister said, "Earth to earth, and ashes to ashes, and dust to dust." Then they went back to the dreary house, the father and mother and Dell. All the rest went away to their work, to their study, to their play. But Dell came back and set the chairs in less formal array and drew up the paper shades and put away in a little box one small wreath that had lain on Mamie's breast — put it with a curl of hair and a little speck of a locket that Mamie had worn and loved. She made a cup of tea and a bit of toast that the poor mother could not eat. Finally she knew she must go home; they would have to take up their burden of living alone. Out on the gate, through which she would have to pass, leaned Sam Miller. She was sorry for that. The stricken mother might have pity in her heart for him, but Dell felt little; her heart was bitter toward him. She did not want to meet him or speak to him. He held open the gate for her to pass. As she was doing so, he stopped her.

"Miss Bronson, I suppose your father can do without me tonight?" he said hesitatingly.

Yes, Dell said, he would not be expected that night.

"There was something else," he said as she was moving on. "I think — I mean — will you tell your father he will have to get someone else to do his work after this? I can't come there anymore."

Dell turned eager, hopeful eyes upon his face. "I am so glad to hear you say so. I have been hoping you would find better work. Where are you going?"

"I don't know," he said. "I haven't got to that yet. I only know what I ain't going to do; and I'll tell you what that is, Miss Bronson, because I think you will be glad to know. I ain't going to touch another drop of rum, so help me God. I promised my little Mamie that, when I was all alone with her a few minutes the night before she died, and I mean to keep the promise. My wife don't know anything about it yet, but Mamie knows, and God knows."

It is impossible to give you an idea of the solemnity of Sam Miller's tone. It impressed Dell with a sense of respect such as she had never before felt for him. Also with a certain sense of awe as if he were being sustained and strengthened by some unforeseen power. She held out her hand to him, having no words to say. He grasped it eagerly and then asked in a quiet, determined voice: "Have you got your pledge book about you, Miss Bronson? I mean to sign the pledge, and I'd like to do it tonight, partly because I shall feel stronger after it's done, and then I think Mamie would like it."

"And your wife," Dell said as she drew forth her unfailing pocket companion, a tiny black-covered pledge book. "Why, Sam, only think what a world of comfort you are going to bring to her sad heart tonight!"

"Yes, it will comfort her. Mamie thought of that too." Then he rested the little pledge book on the post of the gate and wrote with steady hand the name Samuel Miller.

Home through the deepening twilight sped Dell. Home and up to the quiet of her own room. Her heart was in a tremble of thanksgiving and self-reproach. How utterly she had distrusted her Father. With the very weapon which she in her wisdom had felt sure would destroy him, God had spoken to the soul in danger and turned his footsteps. And Dell sought her knees in thankful and repentant prayer.

CHAPTER XVIII

A RENEWED EFFORT

*"My son, give me thine heart,
and let thine eyes observe my ways."*

im Forbes had taken even less pains than usual with his dress — his coat was out at both elbows and very much frayed and soiled at the wrists. He loafed along in a reckless fashion as though he knew he was looking his worst and didn't care. His companion was fresh and dainty in a newly ironed blue and white muslin of delicate pattern, soft filmy laces at throat and wrists; a spray of mignonette shed faint perfume all about her. The conversation on her part was earnest. With him it partook of his general appearance and also seemed reckless.

"When a fellow has give up — why, that's the end, and there's no more use of talking. I tried it — you know I did — and it was no kind of use, and now I've just given up."

"But, Mr. Forbes, I don't believe in any such doctrine, you know. I want you to try again. No one ever accomplished much with once trying."

"Once!" he repeated fiercely. "I've tried a thousand times. You don't know anything about it, Miss Bronson. No woman don't. I thought I'd rather cut my hand off than to break that pledge, and now I've gone and done it, and there's no use in talking."

"Let's act then, instead of talking," Dell said. "You come right down to the temperance meeting with me and sign the pledge over again. Then everybody will see you are in earnest."

Jim shook his head emphatically. "No, ma'am, I ain't a-going to do it. Whatever I be, I ain't the fellow to make promises and go back on 'em and make 'em over again as easy as that. I don't go over all this trouble again for nobody."

"Then," Dell said, with a weary sigh, "you will disappoint me sadly. I trusted you, not because I thought you would get along without failures. I know about the fearful temptations, although you think I do not. You seem to forget where I live and who my father is. But I felt confident you would try again."

Jim Forbes looked down at the sad young face with a respectful curiosity in his gaze. "I'd not disappoint you if I could help it — I'd rather be hanged than do it," he said at last, with a rough attempt at gallantry. "But you see how it is: I can't be anybody, and I ain't going to pretend I can."

"Mr. Forbes, won't you try once more, to please me?"

"And s'posing I do, and fail again?"

"Why, then," said Dell, "I should want you to try again." Whereupon Jim laughed; his bitter spirit was not entirely proof against her brisk tones and words.

"Besides," she said, trying to follow up her advantage, "it is such a wretched time now to desert the field — just when you are needed. Don't you know Sam Miller needs your help?"

"My help!" snorted Jim, all the bitterness returning. "Jolly help I'd be to any poor wretch. And whose help do you s'pose I need to keep me straight while I'm helping others?"

"God's," said Dell.

To which he made no sort of answer. He had long ago ceased sneering at that name, at least in Dell's presence. They walked on a few steps in silence. Meantime Mr. Tresevant and Miss Emmeline Elliot passed them. Dell, intent upon her work as she was, had time to notice the weary, pale look on the clergyman's face and to feel one sharp pang of pity over the desolation of his life and her own, ere she turned again to Jim and asked her earnest question:

"Won't you make another trial rather than disappoint me, Mr. Forbes?"

"I can't do it tonight," he said. "Why, Miss Bronson, you don't know the whole. You wouldn't want me to if you did. I — I've been drinking this very night, and all the fellows know it. If I should go down there, anybody who stood near me would smell rum, and you see how that would look."

"I know all about that," Dell said. "I knew you had been drinking when I first met you. I knew you were on your way to drink more. Do you think people who have been drinking liquor ought not to go to a temperance meeting or make up their minds to sign a pledge? I'm sure they are the very people I am after. As for the breath, I have my pocket full of cloves; they will destroy the smell of whiskey. Mr. Forbes, will you go with me this evening?"

"Yes," said Jim, with a sudden determination in his eye. "Yes, I will. I'll come."

They were very near the church now, and at the door Jim halted. "You go on in," he said gruffly. "I'll come pretty soon."

And Dell, deciding that to be her wisest course, left him. A very respectable audience was gathering. As literary entertainments, the temperance meetings were growing in favor. Dell was at the wheezy organ, playing an interlude during the second song, when Tommy Truman made his way to her side and began an eager story: "Jim Forbes is on the steps, but he will not come in. He's been drinking," Tommy whispered in low, shocked tones. "And he is ashamed. He says all the fellows know about it, and they are coming tonight, and he can't."

Meantime the organist prolonged the interlude, striking chords at random and questioning the troubled little speaker. When she began to sing again she skipped two verses, sang the last, then passed down the aisle out into the hall. Jim lounged in a miserable state of indecision and shamefacedness against the door. She went toward him and spoke rapidly.

"See how much you disarrange our program by your tardiness? I had to skip the opening song and put the second one third because I didn't want to sing it without your bass. Do come in now; it is nearly time for the next singing."

"Miss Bronson — I can't — I vow I can't," said miserable Jim. "You don't know how I feel, and all the fellows are coming. It's no use talking."

Dell turned and looked full in his face with great solemn eyes. "Why, Mr. Forbes, you promised!"

He returned the look, his very hair seeming to

grow redder. At last he muttered, "So I did! Well, Miss Bronson, I'll come," which he presently did, looking flushed and uncomfortable.

Mr. Tresevant, notwithstanding his settled and unwavering objections to the temperance pledge, seemed inclined to haunt the temperance meetings. He and Miss Emmeline Elliot were together this evening, and Dell wished at least one of them was elsewhere.

At the close of the literary exercises Mr. Nelson asked for the forgiveness and reinstatement of one of their number who had broken his pledge but was again among them, repentant and ready to try again. After the pardon of the society was unanimously granted, poor Jim stumbled forward, summoning greater courage for his awful passage from his seat to the pledge table than he would have required to face the cannon's mouth. As he reached the front of the church, Miss Emmeline giggled and whispered to her companion loud enough for both Jim and Dell to hear: "Here comes Miss Bronson's protegé again. Do you suppose they have him sign every time for effect?"

Mr. Tresevant made some inaudible reply and looked very pale. He had not reached the point where he could ridicule anything in the remotest degree connected with Miss Bronson.

As for Jim, he drew himself up with fierce, angry eyes and had nearly laid down the pen when Dell, bending forward from her seat by the organ, murmured low, "I thank you very much, Mr. Forbes." Instantly the pen was grasped again, and the crossed-out name was renewed.

"I think it is very remarkable that you succeeded in prevailing upon that poor fellow to come tonight," Mr. Nelson said as he and Dell walked homeward after the meeting. "Do you know he emphatically refused me today, though I presented every argument and inducement in my power?"

But Dell was sad. She did not feel encouraged. It was well to bear a hopeful face before poor Jim if she could, but in truth her heart was heavy. "I don't know that it will be of any use," she said wearily. "He will probably break his pledge again and be in a worse state than before. I confess I have very little hope of him."

Mr. Nelson eyed her searchingly. "Are you going to desert your colors and lose faith in the pledge at this late day?"

"No, not by any means," she said. "I have all the faith in it that I ever had, and I mean to work for it just as faithfully. But I never believed it could work miracles. And it seems to me there is almost a miracle needed in his case. His background, you know, has not been such as to make even a solemn promise very binding, and his temptations are many. I think the pledge is better calculated to keep earnest-minded young men, those who have conscientious natures. I cannot help thinking there is but one hope for poor Jim. If he had the 'Strong Arm' to lean upon, then his pledge would be kept. But, unfortunately, those weak natures are the very last to submit themselves to Christ. I am as hopeless in regard to that as I am about the other."

"Do you think weak natures are less likely to be religious than stronger ones?"

"Much less. Don't you think weak people are obstinate people? I think they nearly always have a mistaken idea of their own strength, while a really strong nature is always conscious of how little his strength amounts to after all — and what infinite resources out of and above himself he needs to sustain him."

"It is a new idea," he said musingly, "but I see that it might be a true one. I don't know which people you class me among, the weak or the strong," he added, laughing. "But I certainly have a very modest and limited idea of my own power of accomplishing anything."

"I class you among the people who are doing violence to their own consciences, Mr. Nelson. I hope you will forgive me for speaking thus plainly, but I do not understand you. I do not see how you can reconcile it with your nature to live only half a life."

"I do not understand myself," he said, sighing a little. "I sometimes feel greatly disheartened about it all. But, Miss Dell, if I had your 'Strong Arm' to lean upon, I don't think I would descend into the valley of gloom as you and I seem to have done this evening."

"Then why in the world haven't you it?" she asked quickly. "You seem to have a sense of the power that it ought to exert over your life. And you see very distinctly wherein I fail, when my weak foolish heart gets the better of my sense and faith. Why don't you set me a better example?"

He laughed a little at finding his reproof so suddenly turned upon himself. Then, seeing that she waited for an answer, he said, "Perhaps I haven't your confidence in the ability of the 'Strong Arm.' "

"Oh, yes, you have, Mr. Nelson. I think you believe in Christ just as entirely as I do — the intellectual belief, I mean. The only difference between us is that you do not choose to accept Him as your personal Helper."

"But, Miss Dell, don't you see what an inconsistent being you make me appear? Wherein would be the consistency of such a belief?"

"I certainly do not know, Mr. Nelson. Won't you try to discover that yourself?"

And as she said this, Dell mounted the steps of her own home.

CHAPTER XIX

THE WEDDING
AND THE WINE

*"They would not walk in his ways,
neither were they obedient unto his law."*

squire Burton's house, decidedly the most pretentious in Lewiston, was aglow with light. And his family, with the exception of Judge Elliot's, took the lead in the village. On this particular evening the house was more brilliant than usual, and quite a brilliant company was assembled. The occasion: the wedding of Miss Laura Burton to Mr. Chester Elliot.

Among the guests was Dell Bronson — rather to her own surprise, it must be confessed. Dell had never been received with marked favor by the young people of Lewiston, partly because, while it was perfectly right and proper to drink wine and brandy, it was not just the thing to associate on familiar terms with the daughter of a common rumseller. There may have been another reason: The young people of Lewiston did not care to introduce into their society so formidable a rival as the rumseller's daughter bade fair to be.

So Dell had examined the invitation card with somewhat astonished eyes and speculated as to why she was invited. The first query was answered when, on passing the Burton mansion later in the day, the front door suddenly opened and there rushed out an eager young lady followed by a no less eager young gentleman, who stood looking on with watchful eyes while the young lady almost devoured Dell with kisses. The Winthrops of Boston, guests of the Burtons of Lewiston! Dell could imagine Miss Laura Burton's surprise over Helen Winthrop's delight at meeting Dell Bronson again.

It was quite a Bostonian affair on a small scale. There were four bridesmaids, of whom Miss Emmeline Elliot was chief; her attendant was Mr. Leonard Winthrop of Boston. Dell laughed a little over the lady's evident satisfaction at this arrangement and yet felt it was hardly to be wondered at. Mr. Leonard Winthrop was certainly a man to be proud of, if one chose to manifest pride of that sort.

That most interesting feature of bridal parties, the ceremony, was just concluded. The bride, a small pink and white creature, lost some of her pinkness during the said ceremony and was becoming pale and tepid. Everybody had kissed and congratulated her and told everybody else how lovely she looked and how handsome the bridegroom was and how solemn and impressive the ceremony had been, and then the tide set toward the supper table. Thither went Dell and Mr. Nelson with the rest. The supper table was striking and in excellent taste, and the guests were in excellent spirits. Conversation in detached bits flashed up and down the table till a question of the bride produced a sudden lull.

"Will you pledge my health and happiness, Mr. Tresevant?" Her jeweled hand rested daintily on the wine glass while she waited for his answer. Others waited too. Dell, sitting within a few feet of them, could almost hear the throbs of her own heart as she listened for his reply. Very pale and very grave was Mr. Tresevant, but his answer was prompt and courteous.

"It is a most unusual thing for me to make the slightest use of the beverage in question. But at a wedding, and invited by the bride herself, one can hardly refuse." He touched his glass to hers and raised it to his lips; not a single drop did he drink — Dell saw that — but what did it matter that not a single drop touched his lips when, so far as his influence was concerned, he might have drained the glass?

Mr. Nelson was invited next and declined quietly.

Miss Emmeline Elliot arched her eyebrows to their highest as she asked pointedly: "Is it possible, Mr. Nelson, that your pledge will not allow you to wish a bride health and happiness?"

"Miss Elliot, let me assure Mrs. Chester Elliot that I wish her all the happiness this world has to bestow."

"Ah, but you don't do it in the legitimate way. I should accept no such wishes as that, sister Laura. Seriously, Mr. Nelson, do you believe it is wicked to take such a tiny little swallow of wine as custom demands, here at this private table among friends? If one were in a tavern now or some such low place where common people congregate, it would be quite different. Won't Miss Bronson allow you to do even such a little thing for society?"

The insinuations in both of these sentences were coarse and low, but Mr. Nelson answered her with imperturbable good humor: "Miss Emmeline, I am engaged to deliver a temperance lecture in the schoolhouse at Pike's Hollow tomorrow evening. Won't you please come out there and hear me? I don't feel like producing my arguments here before their time. Meantime, society must excuse me for my awful breach of conduct and allow me to continue as the social bore I have been for so many years."

The roses on Dell's cheeks had been very bright during this conversation, but instead of looking annoyed there was a mischievous light in her eyes. They only danced the more brightly when Miss Emmeline, nettled into an utter breach of courtesy, answered sharply: "Well, you certainly have my sympathy, Mr. Nelson. I pity any man who, in this enlightened age, feels himself tied down to some little-boy notion, as absurd as it is childish, about breaking a pledge."

At this particular moment the waiter paused beside Mr. Leonard Winthrop's glass and prepared to fill it. Quick as thought, the gentleman placed his hand over the glass, and his clear, well-bred voice sounded distinctly down the table: "None for me, if you please. I belong to that daily increasing number of young men who have tied themselves down to the little-boy notion of total abstinence. How goes the work here, Mr. Nelson? Is it encouraging?"

Dell did not hear Mr. Nelson's answer. She was engaged in watching the scarlet flush that had mounted to Miss Elliot's very temples. Who could have imagined for a moment that Leonard Winthrop, belonging to the Winthrops of Boston, was a champion of that absurd and babyish fanaticism, total abstinence?

There was one of the company who evidently had no such scruples. This was none other than the bridegroom. Again and again he filled and drained his glass, until others besides Dell and the Winthrops began to grow unpleasantly conscious of the fact that he hardly knew what he was about.

A return to the parlors, it was hoped, would break the spell. But Mr. Elliot was too much at home in his father-in-law's house to wait for an invitation to help himself at the sideboard, and he was too far under the influence of wine to realize his condition.

"If you have the least influence in that direction, I beg you will use it to prevent more open disgrace." Thus said Mr. Nelson as he stood for a moment near his pastor. As he spoke he inclined his head toward Mr. Elliot, who, with flushed face and loud voice, was talking eager nonsense.

The pale face of Mr. Tresevant flushed slightly. "I must beg to be excused. I do not boast of sufficient familiarity with any gentleman to preach him a temperance lecture at the same time I am accepting his hospitality."

Mr. Nelson turned away and sought Dell, who at that moment was standing somewhat apart.

"I am utterly out of patience with that man!" he said.

"What man? Mr. Elliot?"

"No, Mr. Tresevant. Of the two he acts the most like a simpleton. No one expects much wisdom from poor Elliot, especially when he is tempted on every side as he is tonight. But think of a minister of the gospel setting him such an example and standing aloof from him now, composedly looking on, when a word from him might quiet the fire in the poor fellow's brains! Miss Dell, do you wonder that I have little faith in a religion that bears such fruit?"

Dell's voice and manner were very gentle: "Do you really think, Mr. Nelson, that it is because Mr. Tresevant is a Christian that he takes such a strange, one-sided view of the temperance question? Or is that the weak point in his character that Christianity has not yet overcome?"

Mr. Nelson's gloomy face cleared. He smiled down on the bright eyes lifted to his. "I beg pardon. I spoke harshly, I presume. I have some faith left in religion after all. There are other exponents of it than the one of whom we have just been speaking. Shall I tell you of what you remind me just now? A verse in our lesson for next Sunday: 'Charity thinketh no evil.' "

Their conversation was interrupted. The bridegroom came toward them, his tones at once loud and thick: "Are you admiring my wife?" he asked, glancing at a fair-faced, smiling picture that hung near them. "That doesn't begin to compare with one up in the library; she is the very cream of sweetness in that one. Ever see it, Nelson? No! Then come up and see it now — it was that I fell in love with. But you needn't follow my example, you know; too late for that. Come on, friends," he said, raising his voice almost to a shout. "Everybody who wants to see the lady I fell in love with in her prime, follow me."

"Let us go," Mr. Nelson said in undertone to Dell. "The library is farther from the dining room than the parlors are." Others joined them until quite a group gathered in the library, among whom were the Winthrops, Mr. Tresevant and Miss Emmeline. The face they came to study was fair and sweet enough to have been an angel's. Dell looked at the portrait tenderly. There was a troubled expression in the depth of the brown eyes that she had never seen in the original — a suggestion that the young girl had at some time felt a suspicion there might be sorrow in this world, though it had never come to her. A tender pity for the gentle child-wife crept into Dell's heart as she looked from the pictured face to the restless eyes of the husband. How near the very edge of the whirlpool of sorrow seemed this bride! Would not God in His mercy interpose to help her?

One of the company now discovered that the balcony afforded a delightful view of the rising moon, and half a dozen went out to view the wonderful miracle of the fiery world. Dell lingered beside the picture, strangely moved and saddened by the hidden tears in those soft brown eyes. From the window came the sound of merry voices outside, loudest above them Mr. Elliot's.

"Winthrop, what on earth possessed you to grow so broad and so tall both at once? A fellow can't see through you nor around you nor over your head. Hold on, though; I have an idea. I'll occupy a loftier position than you for once in my life — see if I don't. Clear the way, friends. I'm going up to get a nearer view of the sky."

And as he spoke he vaulted to the delicate iron lattice work that surrounded the balcony. It was a wild idea. No sane man would have attempted to poise himself in mid-air on an iron thread after this fashion, and yet a sane man, having in some unaccountable manner found himself there, would have caught at the iron pillar, clung to the lattice below and saved himself in some way. But this man's brains were confused with liquor. He realized neither his folly nor his danger. It was all done in an instant of time — the unexpected spring, the dizzy pitch forward and then the shrieks and wild rushing down the stairs of those who had witnessed the fall. Dell went swiftly and silently down to the bride. A confusion of cries prevailed below.

"What is it all?" the fair creature said, turning to Dell, who suddenly saw that look of vague trouble in the brown eyes. "Someone has fallen, they say. Fallen where? Who is it? Where is my husband?"

In the midst of which appeared at the window Mr. Tresevant's face, deathly in its pallor. "Dell," he said in a low tone, and Dell turned toward him. "Take her away — his wife — get her into the other room, quick; we want to bring him through the hall."

Dell turned back. "Come with me," she said with gentle authority. "I will tell you about it." And the girl, easily led, allowed herself to be drawn into the little room opening from the back parlor and nestled into a chair. She looked up with frightened eyes. "I know something dreadful has happened," she said faintly, "but I tremble so; I would rather you did not tell me now. I'm afraid I'm going to faint. I always do when I am frightened. Won't you just please go call my husband? Tell him I want him, and he will come. Oh, I am fainting."

And Dell, with a deep sigh of relief, saw that blessed unconsciousness steal over her face. She took the tiny creature in her arms and laid her on the couch. There was a physician among the guests, and for him she sought. He was not occupied, as she had supposed he would be, and came at once.

"We will just let her be," he said in answer to

Dell's query. "It is the most merciful thing that could come to her; she will revive soon enough."

"Is there a physician with him?" said Dell.

"Yes, two of them by this time, and no need for either."

"Why?" said Dell, her voice trembling.

"He is beyond their help. He struck his temple on the corner step, and when we got to him he was quite dead. There, Miss Dell, she is reviving; what shall we say to her?"

CHAPTER XX

THE FUNERAL

"Thy way and thy doings
have procured these things unto thee."

here are those to whom we turn instinctively when the house is full of
mourning. They may not be those
who are counted among our intimate
friends when all goes well with us.
But when sudden sorrow seems as if it would overwhelm us, there are certain helpful souls who seem
to know what and how and when to do, and to them
we look. Such a one was Dell Bronson. She had not
been intimate with the Burton family during their
bright days, but no sooner did this stunning blow
crush down upon them than she roused herself from
the position of passive looker-on. In the terrible
night that followed, everyone in the household
learned how thoughtful, helpful and quiet Miss
Bronson could be. When frightened servants and

anxious friends besieged Mrs. Burton with questions, she replied, "Just ask Miss Bronson, will you? She can tell you where it is," or "I will consult Miss Bronson and let you know. She has looked after these things for me."

And Dell, finding herself useful, stayed on, doing all those numberless things that relatives and more intimate friends could not be expected to do. Also the poor little bride clung to her, seeming to find in her quiet strength something like a refuge in which to hide away. Laura would give little answer beyond pitiful groans to the various perplexing and torturing questions concerning the mourning, until Dell, seeing that they were driving her nearly wild, came to the rescue, asked two or three concise questions that could be answered by yes or no and settled the points at issue. After that, when anyone wanted to know what the poor young widow would like, the answer was, "Just ask Miss Bronson. She will find out for you; Laura seems willing to talk with her."

So it came to pass that Dell was much in the darkened room where the widow, who had been a wife for three hours, lay buried among the pillows. Dell was there when Mrs. Burton came in and went toward her daughter with troubled face: "My darling, Mr. Tresevant has called for the third time. Can't you see him now, just a minute? He will want to know your wishes in regard to tomorrow."

The young woman roused herself and turned her wan face to her mother. "Mama, only one thing I am particular about, and you can arrange that for me. I don't want Mr. Tresevant to have anything to do with the services tomorrow." Mrs. Burton stood aghast. Dell paused in her task of bringing order out of the chaos of the toilet table and turned toward her.

"But, my dear daughter, what a strange idea — quite impossible to carry out. He is your pastor, you know."

"That does not make the least difference, Mama. I do not want to see him at all, and I will not hear him say one word tomorrow."

"But, Laura, why? What am I to tell him? You don't realize how very badly this will look."

"Tell him anything you like, and I don't care in the least how it looks. I am tired of looks. I don't care for anything anymore."

"I am sure I don't know what to do," said Mrs. Burton. "Miss Bronson, do you know anything about this strange idea?"

"No, ma'am," said Dell, and her voice sounded hollow and unnatural to herself.

"Laura," pleaded the mother, "you will not insist on this, I know. It will make so much trouble and bad feeling all around. If you had an intimate friend in the ministry it would be different. But Mr. Tresevant has always been so intimate here, and he was Chester's particular friend, you know."

Laura's white lips quivered, but she raised herself on one elbow and spoke more resolutely than before: "Mama, I am entirely resolved on this point. I never want to see Mr. Tresevant again. He was not a true friend to Chester. He had influence over him. He could have kept him from what he knew was a great temptation if he had chosen. There would have been no wine at our wedding but for him. When we talked the matter over and I objected, Chester appealed playfully to him, that he should settle the question. He answered that we certainly had an honored example — that there was wine at the marriage in Cana, and not one earnest word did he speak to help me. Do you think I will have that man speak his empty words over my husband's coffin?"

"Oh, but, my dear, you are beside yourself," argued Mrs. Burton. "Mr. Tresevant knew he had no right to interfere in your affairs. That was a gentlemanly way of saying so. And as for the accident, poor darling child, it was a fall. No one was to blame; no one could have prevented it. Any gentleman might have had the same."

As the mother spoke, the daughter laid herself back among the pillows with a weary sigh. After a little silence the poor girl spoke again: "Mama, you could talk all day and you wouldn't change my mind. I am fully determined. Arrange anything else as you choose. I don't care anything about it. Only remember, I will not have that man say one word."

Mrs. Burton went away in despair, and erelong Emmeline Elliot came in, her face and eyes swollen with weeping. She had not seen her sister-in-law before that day, but she had evidently come now to plead Mr. Tresevant's cause. The young widow listened, or perhaps did not listen, to the eager arguments and expostulating words, returning the invariable answer, "It is no use talking to me, Emmeline. I am fully determined. I told Mama so."

Emmeline turned to Dell. "Is it possible, Miss Bronson, that you uphold Laura in this cruel and unladylike thing?"

It required all her self-control to answer in low, quiet tones: "I have not felt called upon to advise Mrs. Elliot on a point wherein she did not ask my advice. But if she had, I should have said, 'If Mr. Tresevant is in any way connected with this trouble, his own conscience must be weight enough for him to bear. I would not add to it.'"

Then she turned and went out of the room. In but a few minutes she was summoned in haste and dismay. Laura had fainted. Emmeline did not know what to do with her, and Mrs. Burton could not be found. The doctor, having come to make his morning call, followed Dell to the scene of trouble. The next hour was a very busy and a trying one; the frail girl was roused from one long swoon only to sink into another, so like death itself that sometimes their hearts fairly stood still in terror. When at last the doctor left her in a more hopeful state, he sought the mother and delivered his verdict: Mrs. Elliot's nerves had sustained a great shock; her brain was in a very excited condition; there was strong tendency to fever. It was therefore exceedingly important that her slightest fancies be yielded to; her wishes should not be crossed in any way; she must be kept quiet at all hazards. Soon after that Mrs. Burton called for a private conference with Dell, and, with much embarrassment, expressed her desire that Dell communicate with Mr. Tresevant on the delicate subject.

Dell shrank from the task. "Oh, Mrs. Burton! I cannot help him. It is not my place to do so, and I should not know what to say."

"My dear, I think it is eminently your place. You have been so constantly with our poor child since the accident, and you can represent to him her peculiarly nervous state and the fact that she shrinks from hearing his voice in the service — because of his intimacy with poor Chester." Mrs. Burton delicately ignored the fact that this was not the reason. "You see, Mr. Burton's position as an officer of the church makes it an exceedingly difficult matter for him to manage, and I am sure I should never get through it without blundering. Now, my dear Miss Bronson, couldn't you be persuaded to add this to your long list of kindnesses? I assure you we shall never forget how kind you have been to us. And you are so intimately acquainted with him!"

Dell heard only a word here and there of Mrs. Burton's smooth-flowing sentences. She pitied the pale-faced, hollow-eyed young minister who fairly haunted the house of mourning in his eagerness to be of some service. This added blow she knew would be a heavy one. She longed to avert it; failing in that, would it not be less hard to endure coming from her, told gently and with honest sympathy, such as she could give? Thus thinking, she let herself be persuaded. Receiving in silence Mrs. Burton's thanks and assurances of never forgetting her, she went down to Mr. Tresevant when next he called. He came forward to meet her, gave her a cold, trembling hand and said eagerly, "Dell, isn't there anything I can do?"

She shook her head. "Everything is done, I believe, Mr. Tresevant."

Then, by his next question, he precipitated the entire matter. "I wonder when I am to see Mrs. Elliot to make arrangements about the funeral? Can you find out for me? It is quite time I knew what is desired."

Frankness had always been Dell's habit. She knew no other way, so now she spoke quickly, yet with an undertone of tenderness: "Mr. Tresevant, they have sent me down to talk with you about this. Mrs. Elliot is feverish; she shrinks from seeing anyone, you among others, and they want you to make arrangements with Dr. Carswell to have the funeral."

"Dr. Carswell!" he repeated. "I didn't know he was a special friend. What part in the service do they wish me to assign to him?"

"They want him to conduct the entire service. Mrs. Elliot connects you so closely in her mind with her husband that she does not feel able to hear your voice. They would like you to make arrangements with Dr. Carswell and attend the funeral yourself as a personal friend of the family."

Mr. Tresevant stood before her dumb with wonder and with a heavy pain at his heart. What did it all mean? A friend he had certainly been to Chester Elliot, but not more to him than to almost any other young man connected with his congregation. A little influence he had possessed over him certainly, but he hoped he had some influence over all his people. On that principle was he never to be allowed to bury his dead? There was some mystery about all this.

"Dell," he said appealingly, "what does this mean? I don't understand. Won't you explain it?"

Dell stood before him with downcast eyes and glowing cheeks; great tears filled her eyes. She longed to flee her task. How could she further wound the heart that she knew well enough was aching now with a bitter regret? Yet she would not deceive him.

"Mr. Tresevant, you must remember that Mrs. Elliot has undergone a fearful shock and is not yet capable of thinking calmly. She associates you with her husband's condition on the night of the accident; she perhaps exaggerates your influence over him. This much she cannot keep her pitying heart from saying. And so just now it is painful to her to see or hear you."

It was a heavy blow that quivered through the sensitive minister's body. Dell felt it all for him; she longed to clasp his hands, lay her head upon his shoulder and weep out her sympathy. But he didn't know her heart. He didn't see the unshed tears in those brown eyes. He was hurt to his very soul, and he was just as unreasonable as most other sensitive people are when something unexpected has stung them. Besides, he didn't in the least understand the young lady whom he had asked to be his wife. He answered her in tones as cold as ice: "This is evidently your work, Miss Bronson. I hope you may be able to enjoy your triumph with a clear conscience."

Suddenly the tears in Dell's eyes had no disposition to fall. Indeed, they seemed to have burned their way back to their source. Talk of his being hurt — he would never have any conception of how he had wounded her.

If, she said in her heart, if he really, after all that has passed, knows me no better than to think I could do that — what is the use of talking to him at all? She lifted her eyes, stern now and dry, then turned and left the room.

"Have you settled the matter satisfactorily, my dear?" said Mrs. Burton, with both eagerness and nervousness. The impropriety of a rupture with their pastor, at such a time and under such circumstances, was of all things to be avoided.

Dell, jealous for his honor and understanding him better than he did himself, answered quietly: "Yes, ma'am, he understands your wishes. But I think he would like to confer with you concerning the arrangements to be made with Dr. Carswell."

Dell knew he would be his own proud self before Mrs. Burton; the sooner he talked this thing over with the solemn dignity demanded of the occasion, the sooner he would calm down.

But Dell had been stabbed to the heart.

CHAPTER XXI

JIM FORBES'S SPEECH

"I have seen his ways, and will heal him."

 haven't heard a word from him since he went away," Mr. Nelson told Dell as the two walked down the street together toward the church; it was the evening devoted to the temperance meeting. "I used all my influence with Mr. Elliot to send some other fellow and let us keep Jim here under our influence, but I accomplished nothing. Jim happened to be the best man for the sort of work they wanted done, and of course his well-being must not be weighed for an instant against the press of work. I fear the very worst for him; he has gone to a hard place."

"He could hardly do much worse than he was doing here," said Dell. "He broke his pledge three times, you know."

She was discouraged and beginning to feel that she had "toiled all night and caught nothing." Six weeks had passed since that sad funeral, and she had not seen Mr. Tresevant to speak with during that time. She had hoped for so much to come from that painful time. She had imagined that her faith was strong and the way distinct. She had believed that God meant to speak with force and power to the soul of this, His minister, to arouse him to higher views and holier purposes. During all her time in the house of mourning, while mingling her tears of sympathy with the widowed bride, she had felt an undertone of joyful anticipation as she watched and waited for the hour when he would declare himself led by God to look at life from a different standpoint. This hope bore her up during the trying funeral scene when the pastor sat with white, suffering face, apart, listening as a stranger led the service. Her heart bled for him.

"It is cruel," she said under her breath. "He cannot think I had anything to do with it, or if he thinks so today, he will not tomorrow when some of the bitterness is past. I would not have him endure this scene if any word of mine could have helped it." And yet underneath this feeling was that other one, almost exultant: "The Lord whom he serves is leading him, showing him just where he stands. He, a good and sincere man, will come into the full light."

But tomorrow came and went, and Mr. Tresevant went steadily on with his usual work, avoiding her, not seeming to desire even so much as a glimpse of her. Clearly he believed his public disgrace was owing to her, and clearly too he thought only of the disgrace, nothing of the soul that his outstretched hand might have led to safety.

It appeared in time that the disgrace was not much

after all. People remarked how deathly pale Mr. Tresevant was on the day of the funeral; how well it was that he did not undertake to conduct the services, else he would surely have failed. They added that he must have cared more for young Elliot than they had supposed, and then they turned to something else and forgot all about it. So the minister carried in his eyes, whenever he was obliged to meet Dell, a look of proud satisfaction that her scheme to humiliate him had failed. And she knew not what to think; everywhere her work and hopes seemed equally to have come to naught.

So on this particular evening she spoke bitterly, almost indifferently, about Jim Forbes; she did not feel indifferent, only discouraged. Poor Jim had certainly been a discouraging object. Now for six weeks he had been away, sent by Mr. Elliot to help mend broken machinery at another mill in a town, if possible, lower on the social and temperance scale than Lewiston. And Dell felt as hopeless concerning him as Mr. Nelson possibly could, even though she nightly commended him to the "Strong Arm" she firmly believed was "mighty to save."

Tommy Truman met them at the door and to them with eager face.

"Jim Forbes has got back, Mr. Nelson," he claimed when he was within speaking dista

"Has he indeed?" said Mr. Nelson hearti Dell said not a word.

"Yes, sir, and he is coming tonight. He s got something to tell the meeting."

Dell looked up to Mr. Nelson with a "He wants to sign the pledge again, I su they went into the church.

A fair-sized audience was already g

becoming quite the fashion to attend these temperance meetings, the music and literary exercises continuing to be very attractive. Mr. Tresevant and Miss Emmeline Elliot were present. Mr. Tresevant rarely attended the meetings during those days, but some power had drawn him there this evening.

Presently came Jim Forbes down the aisle with steady step and a clear light in his brown eyes. Jim wore a clean shirt and a whole coat that had been carefully brushed; his hair was combed with unusual nicety, and his collar was crisp and white. Altogether, Jim had never looked so well in his life. Trooping down the aisle after him came Dell's entire class, and after them a large delegation of some of the worst characters in the mill. They took their seats noisily. Evidently an unusual interest centered around Jim Forbes, though he could not have been in town more than an hour. He went directly to Mr. Nelson and whispered a few words; Mr. Nelson nodded assent, and Jim quietly took his seat, pausing only to grasp Dell's hand for an instant as he passed the organ. At the conclusion of the literary exercises, Mr. Nelson announced that their friend Mr. Forbes, who had been absent for several weeks, had a few words to say. Jim rose at once and came forward with an air of simple dignity that became him well, and this was the speech he made:

"I don't know how to make a speech. I never made one, but I've got something I want to tell you. I told the boys that if they would come down here with me tonight, I would tell them something. And I wanted to tell the rest of you too. You all know what I've been, and some of you know how hard I've tried lately to stop drinking. I wanted to stop. I meant to stop. When I signed that pledge, I thought I had drunk my last drop, but it wasn't so.

"The pledge helped me a good deal. After I signed it, I went without drink longer than I ever did before since I was ten years old. But I was tempted. And you folks who have never drunk don't know what it is to be tempted in that way. I broke my pledge. I tried to make the boys believe I did it for fun, that I didn't care, but it wasn't so. I felt bad. I can't tell you anything about how bad I felt. I thought there was no use trying anymore, and so I gave up. But I had a friend," and here Jim's voice broke a little, "and that friend came after me and talked to me and coaxed me and wouldn't let me go to the dogs that time, though I seemed to want to bad enough.

"So I tried again, harder than I had before, and you'd be surprised at the lot of folks that wanted to ruin me and how hard they worked for it and how few there were seemed to care whether I was ruined or not. Well, the lot succeeded, and down I went again, and that time I was worse than before. But I had the same friend sticking to me, getting me to promise to try again. Though it seemed to me of no kind of use, I did try, some weeks at a time, and then I tumbled back again.

"Then one night when my boss came and made an offer to go to another town to work, I jumped at the chance. I says to myself, I ain't nobody and I can't be. I've tried as hard as a fellow could, but I was too far gone before I begun. So now I'll go away. I can spree it as much and as hard as I like, and there won't be anybody to feel bad or to coax me or to care what becomes of me.

"So I went away, but who do you think was after me harder than anybody had ever been before? Why, it was the Lord Himself, and He didn't let go of me though I tried to get away. I went into a rum hole, and He followed me and coaxed me out before I took a single drink. I told Him it was no use. I says, 'I've tried it again and again and I ain't nobody and I can't be. Now I've given up for the last time and want to be let alone.'

"And says He to me, 'Jim, that's just the trouble — you've tried "it" but you never have tried Me — never. "It" is a good help, but you are too far gone. You want something stronger — you want something so strong that you can't get away from it. You want more than that — something so strong that you can't want to get away from it. Try Me, Jim. Try Me.'

"And it flashed all over me that this was the solemn truth. I just stood still there in the street in the dark, and I says, 'O Lord, I will.' And I did. And all the while I was to work in that mill, going up and down those streets, passing hotels and saloons and cellars by the dozen. He never left me a single minute — not a minute. I didn't even want to go into one of them places; I shrunk away from them; I hated them. I worked against them all the time. I didn't feel afraid I should go back to them anymore, for I could feel that the Lord had tight hold of me. And now I am His."

Here Jim paused in his speech and drew out his handkerchief. There seemed to be need for many handkerchiefs around the church just then.

"I've just one thing more to tell the boys," he began after a moment. "If they really want to get away from the rum — or even if they don't want to and are willing to be coaxed into wanting to — He's the Friend and Helper to come to. The pledge is good; it helped me. But God is stronger than the pledge, and some of us need just the strongest kind of help we can get. Come and try my Friend. You don't know anything about Him, and it's little I can tell you. But I can feel His power, and so can you if you want to.

"Now I want everybody to know," and Jim drew himself up with strange dignity, "I belong to the Lord — body and soul. I'm going to live for Him and work for Him, but there's something more important than all that: He's going to work for me."

There was a solemn silence in the room after Jim took his seat. The boys from the mill were quiet and grave. They marveled greatly, as if one of their own had been speaking in an unknown tongue.

Mr. Nelson rose and stood for a moment in silence. Then his voice broke the stillness: "Our friend has proved forcibly tonight that his help is in God. He said, 'Some of us need just the strongest kind of help we can get.' I want to vary that statement a little and express my solemn conviction that *all* of us need just that kind of help — and that it is found alone in God. I honor the total abstinence pledge. I believe it to be one of God's chosen instruments of usefulness. But I have been slowly turning from my early bulwark, that man needed but to use the strength inherent in his nature to be what he would. I feel that I need God. And I hereby pledge myself and all that I have and am and hope to be to His service from this time forth. Let us pray."

"I thought you would be happy tonight," Mr. Nelson said gently to Dell as they walked homeward, "and here you are in tears. What's the matter?"

"I am weeping over my own folly," she answered, smiling a little through her tears. "Though I pride myself on being a daughter of the King, it seems I cannot trust Him to do His own work in His own time and way. I seem determined to insist on choosing my time and my way, and when I fail, discouragement and depression seize upon me as if the cause were lost."

CHAPTER XXII

THE FIRE

*"And the Lord went before them
by day in a pillar of a cloud, to lead them the way;
and by night in a pillar of fire."*

It was after eleven o'clock when Dell, on her way to her room, paused before the barroom door. Hearing no sound within, she ventured to open it and peep in. Such a contrast that room presented to the rest of the house, which had long since come under Dell's sway. Cleanliness and order prevailed, and evidences of a refined and cultured taste were gradually taking up their abode in every room. Everywhere but in the barroom. The more comfortless and forlorn and dirty that place could be made to look, the better pleased was Dell.

On the evening in question she peeped cautiously in. Six or seven loungers were flopped in chairs or disposed along the wooden settees, and every one of them was asleep. The close air, the smoking stove and lamps, together with the intolerable smell of tobacco and bad whisky had been too much for them; their snores were becoming every moment more distinct and determined. Seated just in front of the smoldering fire, Mr. Bronson slept, tipped back in one of the hard chairs, his slouched hat pushed to one side. How old and worn he looked! Dell had never before noticed how sunken his cheeks were, how very gray he was. Wasn't it incredible that a man as old as he, as tired as he must be, should prefer to sit sleeping in that hard chair in the filthy room when there awaited him a bed as soft and white and sweet-smelling as careful hands could make it? Every day the wonder grew upon Dell.

Every day the house took on a daintier aspect, and her father seemed to appreciate and enjoy it. Oftener he came and longer he lingered in the fair morning room that she had made for his special entrapment. Yet what did it amount to since he daily increased his capacity and his passion for whiskey, so that often he came and sat down in her cushioned chairs and profaned the purity of that fair room with ceaseless spittings and even oaths? All to no purpose looked the sacrifice of Dell's life; her father had set up an idol in his heart long ago, and every day he bestowed more of his heart's love on it. Every passing day seemed to make it more improbable that he would ever seek any other love. Yet, looking upon him, Dell daily said over to herself this unalterable promise: "I know the thoughts that I think toward you, saith the Lord; thoughts of peace, and not of evil, to give you an expected end." She shut the door softly upon that disgusting scene and went up the stairs singing to herself:

God moves in a mysterious way,
His wonders to perform.

Actually singing — while her drunken father slept in that dreadful barroom. You see, she had an expected end. Dell had risen into a higher plane of life during these passing months. With her, in a sense, hope had been lost, not in fruition but in expectation. Why? Because of the promise — rather, the long chain of promises, link after link of which she knew by heart; on each separate link she fed herself, reminding the King daily, hourly, of His own words. She knew they were of more importance to Him than half His kingdom, and she knew His scepter was held out to her, so now she just waited in daily expectation of the end that she knew was to come.

How? Ah, that she did not know. Moreover she had given up trying to know. Not given up trying to help, you understand. Not a bit of that. She held on to her end of the chain. She spread her little traps and snares and looked eagerly to see if her father would fall into them; she wondered if that would be the way by which the end would come. And as he chose one by one apparently to ignore her ways, she told herself that God's ways were not as her ways, nor His thoughts as her thoughts. Realizing how infinitely higher and better His ways must be than hers, she put her hand in His and trod bravely on. Certainly this daughter of the King had learned one lesson during all her time of humble waiting, worth all the hours of discipline that it had required — the lesson of patient, prayerful trust. She went briskly about preparing for the night's rest; the hour was late.

But late as it was, she dived down into the bottom of an unpacked trunk in search of a thick wrapper lined with flannel that she had determined should go with Mrs. Cooley's bundle in the morning. Mrs. Cooley was sick, and the winter was severe. Dell had been sewing all that day getting ready some comfortable garments for the sick woman. It was part of this girl's method of preaching the gospel, and it also belonged, perhaps, to the doctrine of retribution — that while the father sold Jack Cooley all the whiskey he would drink, the daughter struggled faithfully to replace to the wife and children some of the comforts stolen by the whiskey.

Two hours later she had peacefully drifted off to Boston, having a delightful talk with Uncle Edward, when she was suddenly jolted back to Lewiston; she sat up in bed with bewildered vision and startled ears. What had she heard to awaken her so suddenly? She wondered — only for an instant, as the words rang out: "Fire! Fire! Fire!" caught up and repeated from mouth to mouth. She sprang up and looked out on the village from each window. She saw no visible sign of blaze but rather people running toward the hotel. A vigorous pounding and loud calls were heard at the front door! One glance into the smoky hall revealed the secret. In an instant she enveloped herself in the woolen wrapper she had been at such pains to find and rushed downstairs to draw the bolts of the front door.

In poured the townsmen ready and eager for work. The next hour became a maze of bewilderment to Dell. She knew she worked — tore up and down stairs, brought blankets to wrap around her father and the six with him. She knew they were rescued at infinite risk and that Sam Miller and Jim

Forbes were foremost in the work. She knew she brought keys and unlocked doors to save the time it would take to burst them open. Finally, she remembered coming downstairs with her Bible and her watch and Mrs. Cooley's bundle and following her father across the way to Widow Parker's. But all her movements were mechanical and unreasoning.

In the course of time she realized that her father had been badly wounded, that he was lying on the bed and that she was to take care of him. The doctor had been there and dressed his wounds and given him morphine. While he slept, still unaware of much that had been, Dell stood by the window and watched the men across the way, working like soldiers in a battle. And she saw plainly enough that in another two hours there would not be a beam or a plank left of the old tavern. Even at that solemn hour a strange feeling of exultation came over her. No more whiskey would ever be sold there! Her father had drunk the last drop he would ever get at that bar. And then what barrels of the poison were being made away with, licked up by the wild flames — so much more reasonable it looked than to see men swallowing it.

Again came to her those two lines:

> God moves in a mysterious way,
> His wonders to perform.

She did not sing them this time, but she thought them as she stood at the window and watched the house melt away. Presently she spoke aloud and solemnly: "This is His way, is it? Well, burn."

Before evening of the next day Dell had reason to feel that the rum was not all licked from earth by the night's flames. Her miserable father lay on his bed unable to move hand or foot but able to speak, and his constant cry was "whiskey!" Burning with fever, suffering in every nerve, realizing that the ill-gotten gains of years had perished in half a night, this one desire was yet strong enough to overreach all others. "Something to drink. Something to drink."

In vain Dell prepared and brought this and that cool liquid and held them temptingly before him. He wanted none of them. Something strong, something to build him up — this was his constant groan. Everybody with whom she came in contact conspired against her. Wise ones gravely shook their heads and said it was wrong to cross him so; he was accustomed to stimulus, and he must have it or he would die. Even Mr. Nelson, who called in the course of the day. When Dell pitifully appealed to him for encouragement, he said he did not know; he was not skilled in these things. Perhaps, since he had always been accustomed to it, it might be dangerous to irritate him so; yet he should very much dislike to give him stimulus if he had it to decide. At the same time it was hard to go contrary to everyone's opinion, physician and all. On the whole he did not know anything about it; it would be impossible to tell what he would do if he were similarly situated.

Throughout the long, weary day Dell stood resolutely on guard, resolute outwardly at least, but with such a troubled heart. What was the right thing to do? Could she possibly bring herself to give him a drink of that hated poison after having spent so many hours in prayer for his release from its dominion? In the early evening they were having another debate on the same question: the dapper little doctor, who was Dell's special dislike, and she; Mr. Nelson standing apart, an interested and troubled listener, and Jim Forbes, an eager and excited one.

"Now I tell you, Miss Bronson," Dr. Jones said pompously, "you can't make the world over in a minute, even if it would be well to do so at all. Your father has been used to a drink of whiskey every day, and whiskey he must have or he will die, as likely as not. Anyway, this chafing and fretting are very bad for him. You can certainly see that."

"But I thought whiskey was not advisable by anyone during a fever," said Dell.

"But, my dear Miss Bronson, the fever is doubtless the result of this day's constant fretting. I would not wish to over-urge you, but the consequences of this strange fancy on your part may be serious."

If only she could trust him, could be sure he knew what he was talking about. If only she knew what was the right thing to do! She looked wearily over toward Jim Forbes, standing in the corner. He stepped forward a little, emboldened by her attention.

"I wouldn't give him liquor, Miss Bronson," he said.

The doctor wheeled around on him with an angry air. "Perhaps you would be willing to undertake the case," he said with a sneer.

Dell interposed. "I am not convinced that it is the best course to feed my father on what has been his lifelong curse. Until I am, I shall not give him whiskey."

"Young lady, would you like your father to die?" asked Dr. Jones in his sternest tones, which truth to tell were not very stern, for dignity and sternness were not his forte. The thought, not the words, paled Dell's face. Could she have her father die as he had lived, drinking away his senses, lulled into his last sleep with that awful rum? And yet was her action periling his life? She seemed hunted on every side. A slight bustle in the hall arrested Dr. Jones's attention. Dell had not noticed it, but when the door opened she raised her eyes. A tall, handsome form, a gentle, manly, trustful face — one glance and Dell sprang forward with something between a laugh and a sob, "Uncle Edward! I knew you would come."

"My darling," he said in that voice of fatherly tenderness. "How is he tonight?"

And Dell held up her head and her thoughts went back to her father. "He is worse, I'm afraid. Must I let them give him whiskey?"

"We will try to determine that very soon. My dear, do you see my companion?"

A tall, gray-haired man stepped a little out of the shadow, and Dell's face lighted with a sudden hope and gladness such as even her uncle's coming had not brought. She held out both hands to him and said, "Dr. McHenry!"

CHAPTER XXIII

THE DOCTORS AND THEIR PATIENT

His ways are not as our ways.

t seemed to be a magical name, "Dr. McHenry." Dr. Jones drew himself up and bustled forward, and Mr. Nelson bent searching eyes on the newcomer. The name was very well-known in Lewiston, though Lewiston had never before laid eyes on the great man. "The five-hundred-dollar Boston doctor," he was called, by reason of the many fabulous stories afloat concerning his marvelous cures and equally marvelous prices. Fable aside, he was undoubtedly a wonderful doctor, and the joy in Dell's eyes did not compare with the sudden relief in her troubled heart. Dr. Jones was promptly introduced and the question of whiskey or no whiskey again presented.

"I can form no opinion until I see the patient," said

the Boston doctor. So daughter, uncle and physicians went to the patient's room, the two others remaining outside, eager for the conclusion of the whole matter. After a rapid examination of the patient's pulse and a few brief questions, Dr. McHenry fixed his gray eyes on the local doctor's face and said: "It seems to me there is plenty of febrile action already. I see no occasion for increasing it."

"Of course not," agreed the little doctor, "and in ordinary cases I should not advise it. But the excitement of the patient is such that I thought it better to allay it with a very little of what he craves."

"Suppose his diseased stomach should choose to crave a dose of arsenic. What then?" Very low, very grave was the question, and the gray eyes were fixed thoughtfully on the man.

Dr. Jones crimsoned and made haste to answer: "Of course, we wish your advice in the matter. I have felt the need of consultation myself. I have no doubt you are right, but the excitement, my friend. I assure you he has been perfectly raving for liquor all day. How would you manage that?"

"I should not hope to allay it by feeding him whiskey."

At this point the sick man roused from his uneasy slumber and began his petition for a drop of something cooling and strengthening. Meantime the Boston doctor had withdrawn into the shadow, motioning his companion to do the same. Dell offered her earnest explanation why it was impossible to gratify him, to which he responded with impatient and contemptuous exclamations. Dr. Jones bustled up to him and offered his crumb of comfort: "We have decided, Mr. Bronson, that the nervous condition of your system is such that we shall have to refuse you all liquors for the present."

"Nervous, fiddlesticks!" said Mr. Bronson in feeble anger. "When did you decide it? Seems to me you've wonderfully changed your mind. You told me not an hour ago that it would do me good to have a drink."

"Not quite that, Mr. Bronson," replied Dr. Jones, still crimson. "But since that time we have had a consultation and decided differently."

"Who has?"

"Dr. McHenry, of Boston."

Mr. Bronson knew the name very well indeed. For about half a minute he was awed and astonished; the next he clearly believed Dr. McHenry to be a myth, so far at least as his presence in Lewiston was concerned.

"I don't care for all the doctors in Boston put together," he said. "I want a drink, and I'm going to have it."

Dr. McHenry stepped forward quietly. "Let me try," he said to Dr. Jones, fixing those singular gray eyes on the patient and speaking in clear, steady tones: "My friend, are you entirely ready to die?"

A sudden shiver ran through Jonas Bronson's frame, and for once his attention was turned from whiskey. "Are you Dr. McHenry?" he asked in an awed tone.

"I am," and then the doctor repeated his question, the steady eyes reading the sick man's face.

Mr. Bronson's voice grew husky and trembled over his next question: "Am I going to die?"

"That is more than I can tell you, but I can state the case frankly. You have burnt up your stomach with rum; that is much worse to manage than the burns on your body and makes things more serious for you. At the same time, if you will aid us like a man in our efforts by trying to understand that whiskey, in all its forms, is your worst enemy, and if you will undertake the work of trying to keep your mind calm and quiet, we propose, with God's help, to see you safely through your trouble. But if you persist in fretting yourself into a fever over a poison that you must not have, or if anyone is so cruel as to bring you liquor, and you are so insane as to drink it, your life will not be worth that."

An emphatic snap of Dr. McHenry's thumb and finger gave point to this startling sentence, and the mind of Mr. Bronson was most effectually set at rest on the liquor question.

The days that followed were full of sickening anxiety. The patient had drained his constitution years before and had very little left with which to endure his pain. Added to his torment was the burning of a perpetual craving thirst that refused to be allayed by anything within his call. Still Dr. McHenry's words had thoroughly sobered and frightened him, and he gave what strength he could to smother his longings and control his unsteady brain. As for Dell, her faith had returned to her; she did not let it go again for an instant. When her Uncle Edward told her gently: "Dear child, you must be prepared for the worst; Dr. McHenry thinks the case more than doubtful," she looked up in his face with a brave smile and said: "He will not die, Uncle Edward. God will not let him die until he is safe."

Firmly she clung to her belief, even on the fifth day when he seemed to sink beyond all human aid. In answer to a beseeching telegram, Dr. McHenry came again. Arriving late in the day, he tiptoed to the bedside and stood with the rest awaiting in solemn silence the departure of a soul. Even then Dell's face was calm and hopeful. When Mr. Nelson called, in answer to his inquiry she said, "They think he is dying, but he is not."

Later, when the danger had passed, Dr. McHenry said, "I never saw one apparently so near death's door. I had no idea he would ever speak again."

"That was very powerful medicine that we administered," Dr. Jones replied, rubbing his hands in satisfaction.

"It was not medicine that called him back," said Dr. McHenry. "It was the prayer of faith."

God had given Dell in her inmost heart the assurance that her father should not die until that "thought" that He had "toward her" — to give her "an expected end" — was accomplished.

With this assurance she believed that the almost departed soul had been bidden to tarry for a very short time, long enough to hear and accept the pardon at the eleventh hour. Not so; gradually there came to her the knowledge that her share of the work was not yet done. The father was to live indeed, probably for years, though crippled and deformed, needing her constant care and thought, needing to be watched over, fed and cared for like a child. But her father exhibited no childlike gentleness to make the work pleasant and hopeful. As the weeks passed, the excitement and deep interest that had been awakened in the hearts of the neighbors died quietly out.

The village was no longer put in a flutter over Dr. McHenry's comings and goings; the great man had done his work and came no more. Uncle Edward still came, spending one afternoon every fortnight with his child, strengthening her and helping her, and by means of his ample purse gradually making the two rooms that they occupied at the Widow Parker's into bowers of beauty.

Mr. Nelson and Jim Forbes and Sam Miller were patient, faithful, constant friends, yet still the weight of the work and the burden rested on Dell. And heavy the burden certainly seemed. Never in his most hopeless liquor-drinking days had Mr. Bronson been more fully determined to hear not a single word of a religious nature. Indeed his indifference seemed to have been changed into positive vindictiveness. He would not listen to a prayer from his brother-in-law. He would not allow Dell's Bible to be kept on the little stand at the foot of his bed. He stopped her harshly if she began what he called one of her "psalm tunes," and in every way he seemed to have gone backward.

In every way save one: His brain was entirely clear from liquor during these days. Dr. McHenry's final warning had been too plainly worded for even him to disregard, yet he seemed bent on having vengeance for his marvelous self-denial — by being as miserable in himself as possible and making all around him share his misery. Dell was completely shut in from the outside world. No more church-going for her. Her Sunday school class passed quietly into Mr. Nelson's hands, being quite willing to become his pupils if their doing so would be any sort of comfort to Miss Bronson. The temperance meetings still went on, but without Dell.

"It is a good thing," she said to Mr. Nelson one evening, after he had given her an account of a successful meeting and the addition of two new members from her class. "It is a good thing to discover that the earth can turn on its axis without your help, especially when you have been imagining that you did a great deal of the pushing."

On the afternoon of a wintry day, she stood with her uncle in the hall. He was drawing on his gloves, buttoning his overcoat and otherwise preparing for his snowy walk to the train. How she hated to see him leave.

"Doesn't the little heart ever quail just the least bit?" he said, looking down on her and holding her chin in his hand. It had been an unusually hard afternoon. Mr. Bronson had been in his bitterest mood. The Boston merchant had felt such a dismal sense of contrast between the life his darling now lived and the shielded, nurtured life she had lived in Boston; he fairly longed to carry her back into the brightness.

She looked up wistfully. "No, Uncle Edward, at least not often; not when I lean on the Father for strength. You are almost discouraged, I think, but I am not. Do you know I would rather have this intolerance of the whole subject than the absolute indifference that possessed him so long? I think almost any phase of the heart is better than indifference."

"You are right," he said. "An angry conscience is often an aroused conscience. Well," as the time for the train drew near, "good-bye, dear child. God bless and keep you and give you the desire of your heart. What are you especially resting upon today?"

She repeated it with a wistful light in her eyes, "His ways are not as our ways." With hopeful tenderness her uncle added, "His ways are always right."

She stood at the window and watched him as he sped down the snowy street, the man who had been to her a father. Only a moment did she give herself the luxury of looking after him with longing eyes. She turned and went back to the waiting father inside, stilling her heart in the meantime with the thought that watching over and caring for them all was that other Father, whose daughter she really was.

CHAPTER XXIV

THE
ANNOUNCEMENT

*"Great and marvellous are thy works, Lord God Almighty;
just and true are thy ways, thou King of saints."*

he October day was aglow with beauty. All the leaves had adorned themselves with scarlet and crimson and gold, and the leaf-strewn earth rustled gaily as a woman trailed her garments along the walk. Over all, the magnificent sun poured his yellow glory. It was just that time of high carnival that the world takes on before it spreads its gray and naked arms abroad, proclaiming that winter is at hand.

Dell had been out into all the beauty, drinking it in and gathering great bunches of leaves. She had come in and dropped herself on a low ottoman, letting the leaves shower around her while she set herself about arranging them into many colored bouquets. The side door stood open, letting in the breezy freshness of the afternoon. An open fire burned in the grate to dry and sweeten the October air.

Dell wore her favorite dress of snowy white. It was late in the season for white dresses, and Lewiston people thought her absurd. But Dell, hopelessly indifferent to what people thought about her garments, said that black dresses and winter would come soon enough. Every bright afternoon she robed herself in white and compromised with the season by adding a scarlet sash that matched the leaves in her hair and in the vases all about her.

Very happy and bright looked Dell on this particular afternoon, a sweet and settled peace shining in her eyes. Not a day older seemed she on that first afternoon in August more than three years ago. The room in which she sat accorded well with her appearance — bright, fresh and beautiful. And simple, of course, to be in keeping with the low ceiling and the old-fashioned doors and windows, but fairly alive with comfort and in exquisite taste. There was only one large piece of furniture in the room and that a chair, elegantly upholstered, and in this chair, his slippered feet on the cushioned footstool, rested Dell's father. On his face change was distinctly marked; indeed you would hardly have imagined that smoothly shaven, neatly dressed man could be the red-faced drunken man who slept with his slouched hat pushed to one side and his feet tilted above his head on that memorable evening of the fire.

"Father," Dell said, holding up a bunch of the brightest leaves, "did you ever see anything prettier than that?"

"Yes," he said in a fond voice, looking beyond the

leaves to the bright face back of them. "They're wonderful pretty, but I've seen something a great deal prettier."

Dell laughed a happy little laugh; the flattery, broad and absurd as it was, was sweet to her hungry heart. This man, her father, watched her in pleased silence for a few minutes, then said, "You may bring me the Book if you will, child, and I'll read a bit." Dell brought forward a small stand, made to slip inside the wheeled chair, and thereon she placed the handsomely bound, large-print Bible. Adjusting the glasses that the shriveled hands had not strength to arrange, she went back to her work. She had meantime procured a large book for herself and now gave her attention to the selection of the prettiest leaves for pressing, stealing occasional loving glances at the old man bending over "the Book."

Great and marvelous indeed had been the changes wrought in that past year! "His ways" are wonderful indeed. Through much suffering and many disappointments, after dark days of hope deferred, the "expected" end had come, and Dell watched as her father read with reverent face the Bible stories so new and precious to him. Dell's life was bright during these days. With the constant care and prayer that she had bestowed on her father, her heart had been filled with a great and overpowering love — stronger than any filial love she had ever imagined. During recent months the love had been accompanied by a feeling of reverence, almost awe, as the babe in Christ had sprung into higher knowledge and stronger faith than she had attained. As she looked at him, she realized that every gray hair in that bent head was dearer to her than her own life. Looking at him and thinking of the changes in his life, she reflected back over her own past — her hopes and plans and disappointments and victories.

No, said Dell to herself after a moment's earnest thought. I have tried to work hard and accomplish a great many things, but I believe I have done none of them. Well, what difference does it make? Many of the very things I wanted have been done, and if the King has accepted my trying and done the work Himself, what is it to me so long as the work is done?

There were some things not yet done. There was Mr. Tresevant. Dell thought of him, but without sadness. He would come into the light yet — she felt certain of it. The cloud still rested between them; he had never forgiven her for the slight he still chose to think she had brought upon him. She had never seen him alone for a moment since that time, and during his very rare calls on her father he had been only coldly polite to her. Dell waited for the day when he would understand everything in its true light. She did not know how it was to be brought about; perhaps some chance word of his would give her an opportunity to explain. Some way, she could not tell how, it would all come right.

She had lost all her hard, bitter feelings toward him. She had even come to the point of justifying his suspicion of her and looked forward to the days when they, having come fully to understand each other, would talk over these dark days of separation. About the main point that had separated them she had not a doubt; with every passing day new men were coming to the front to aid in the temperance warfare. Mr. Tresevant was too good a man to remain long in the shadow. Once convinced that he had done her injustice, he would be the first to admit it frankly. Then, loving her entirely even as she did him, he would be led to look into the matter with all his heart. Once convinced, nothing would keep him from standing up firmly for the right. Thus reasoned Dell, who watched with every passing day for the time to come. "Perhaps this is the very day that is to set things right. And then — who knows but that God may join us together after all?"

She said it to herself on this particular afternoon, adding out loud to her thoughts, "Perhaps he will come today to visit Father, and that may be the beginning of his change of heart. Someday I will frankly say to him, 'You did me very great injustice that time. Don't you know you did?' And then I shall explain it all to him. I would have done it long ago if he had given me a chance. It was a good while ago, more than a year now. But he will not be in this afternoon — I remember now; he is in Boston, visiting with the Burtons. I wonder why they went to their townhouse so early this year? Poor Laura!" Dell drew a little sigh, as she could not help doing when she thought of that fair young widow and how the brightness of her brief married life went out in such awful gloom.

Something about Laura made her think of Mr. Nelson, but she did not like to think of him during these days; a very sad thing had come to pass. It was nearly three weeks since he had called on her. It was after her father had been made comfortable for the night. She had been so glad to see Mr. Nelson in their cozy parlor; she admired and liked him so much. She had shown her pleasure so openly, but he had overwhelmed her. In all their glad meetings together it had never occurred to her that he was looking forward to her being his wife. When he told her so, in his frank, hopeful way, it smote her heart with a great grief. She felt she had led him astray in her carelessness. She made all the reparation in her power. She told him gently and humbly of her preoccupied heart — that she loved another — and of a certain trouble that came between them, but of her hope and belief that it would be cleared away. In short, she made him her confidant — as she realized now that she ought to have done long before.

Her confidant, except that she spoke no name and gave no definite account of the trouble. But after a painful silence he had suddenly said: "Is it Mr. — ?" Then as suddenly he stopped and blushed to his very temples. "I beg your pardon. I have no right. I thank you, Miss Dell, for your confidence. Some other time I can talk with you. Good night." And he vanished.

That was three weeks ago, and she had not seen him since. Just then occurred a break in her reverie. Tommy Truman called with the mail — the daily papers that Uncle Edward always sent. Tommy was in haste; no time for a chat, so Dell, her father being still absorbed in his reading, unfolded the crisp sheet and glanced down the column of daily news, skimming one item after another until suddenly her eyes were riveted. Twice she read over the familiar words: "In Boston, October 23, at the residence of the bride's parents, by Rev. J.C. Holbrook, D.D., assisted by Rev. Chester Tremain, D.D., Rev. Carroll C. Tresevant, of Lewiston, to Mrs. Laura Elliot, only daughter of Robert Burton, of this city."

The paper lay very still in Dell's lap. She folded her hands above it and stared into vacancy — sat for she did not know how long. When she roused again the sunlight had disappeared. Thick, leaden-colored clouds were over the sky. Some of her leaves had dropped near the grate and been withered by the fire. They rustled and broke underneath her feet as she rose and trod on them. She took her little hearth broom and swept them all into the grate. They blazed up for a moment and then smoldered and died out. Dell shivered; the room was cold. She closed the door and added more coal to the grate.

"Dell, my child," said her father, looking up from his book, "do you remember the night I got you to come into that room over there and sing for us wretches, and you sang a hymn?"

"Yes, Father, very well, indeed."

"Well, do you know, child, I really believe it was then that your old father began to think. You thought I was 'most asleep, but I wasn't, and you thought I went on from bad to worse after that, and maybe I did. But, for all that, you put words into my head that night that I never got rid of, day or night afterward, drink as hard as I could, and the Lord used them very words to bring me to myself at last."

Dell came over without speaking a word and wound her arms around her father's neck. She laid her soft brown head against his gray one. He would never know what balmy words he had been speaking, nor how her sore heart needed them.

"Look here, child," he said, leaning forward again to the Book. "I've found a verse for you and me. I'll read it, and you see if it ain't exactly so. I never came to that verse before." And in slow, tremulous tones he read: "And I will bring the blind by a way they know not; I will lead them in paths that they have not known; I will make darkness light before them, and crooked things straight. These things will I do unto them, and not forsake them."

Dell drew a quick breath. "Yes, Father," she said,

"it is for us." She had "come to" this verse before, but it had never so come to her.

As she drew the shades and lighted the lamp and went about her father's tea and toast, she whispered it over and over, "I will make darkness light before them, and crooked things straight. These things will I do unto them, and not forsake them."